UNDERGRAD

By Christine R. Thibodeau

Dedicated to all parents who are keeping their promise.

Ty was riding a wave as he entered his freshman year of college with a spot on the football team. He was fated to have an extraordinary undergrad experience… But no one could have predicted the journey he was about to take.

Cover photo by Goel Parboo
Author photo by Aristeo Torres

FRESHMAN YEAR

Chapter 1- August Freshman year

Ty, a new freshman, stormed into the university's counselling office. He found no one at the reception desk, so he barged into the first office he found with an open door. He took one look at a man sitting at his desk and proceeded to shout at him, "Who the hell are you and what the !*&!*& is going on?!" Ron looked up from his paperwork and silently stared at Ty for a moment, then returned to his reading.

"Excuse me, I asked you a question!"

Ron looked up again, then down again.

Ty exhaled loudly in exasperation and left the office, slamming the door behind him.

A few minutes later, he knocked at the door.

"Come in."

Ty walked in, his face no longer red and contorted.

"I'm sorry. I see you're demanding respect and all that. Did you get your training from my mother?"

All that followed was silence as Ty kept his gaze steady on Ron.

"Ok, sarcasm not allowed either, sorry. How can I get you to tell me what's going on?"

"Well, you can start by introducing yourself. A handshake would help, too."

Ty looked Ron in the eyes and extended his hand. Ron took it. "I'm Ty."

"Nice to meet you, Ty. You can call me Ron. Swearing will not be tolerated on my turf. I need confirmation that you heard me and will comply."

"Yes, I'll do my best."

"That sounds non committal."

"Ok, I will not swear in your office," Ty mumbled as he sat down.

"That will work for now. What do you want to know?"

"WHAT DO I WANT TO KNOW?!?!"

Ty got up and started pacing. Then, he sat back down and looked at Ron. He took a deep breath.

"Ok, I'm calmer now. Why aren't my parents answering their cell phone? They both recorded a robotic message saying, 'Ty, we'll be ready to talk with you after you've met with Ron.' And, what the hell is this letter?" He waved a piece of paper in front of him.

"I understand this is hard for you, Ty. I need you to listen before you react or cut me off. Can you do that?"

"Yes."

"Like they say in the letter, Ty, they have promised to pay your tuition, room, and board for the next four years. They have one condition. That you agree to see me once a month during this time and cooperate fully with the therapy."

Ty cut Ron off. "Oh, my God. Are you KIDDING ME? That's extortion!"

Silence.

"WHO DOES THIS!?! THEY'RE CRAZY!!!"

Pause.

"They just want to get rid of me, just like that? Like I was still a foster kid, 'dump him off once he turns eighteen'?"

"I doubt that, Ty. They're paying for your entire college education. They're hoping that over the next four years you can… let's say…gain a change of perspective, and find inner peace."

"Well, I'm not some kind of science experiment! I'm not gonna jump through their micromanaging hoops!"

"You don't have to figure out everything all at once. But you will have to come back next month if you want to live up to your part of the bargain. You can call or e mail me in the meantime, or you can come to the office if you set something up with Carla. You don't have to go through this alone."

"That's a laugh! I am alone in this. No one else does this to their kid!"

Pause.

"Please, just talk to my mom. She'll change her mind once she finds out how freaked out I am."

"I'm sorry, Ty."

"You're not sorry! You're helping her pull off this crazy plan!"

"I wonder why you're referring just to your mom and not your dad."

"You've met her… you and I know it's all her. My dad is much more go with the flow. He wouldn't be cruel just to teach me a lesson."

"A lesson…?"

"She's trying to get my attention. That I treat her bad."

"Badly?"

"Yes, Mr. Grammar."

Ty rose to look out the window.

"Ok, I get it; that was a funny joke. It's all a joke. They're hiding in this closet, right?"

Ty looked toward the coat closet.

Silence.

"No, Ty. They're serious."

"NO!"

For a few moments, Ty wiped away tears and then tried to steady his breathing. He turned around and looked intently into Ron's face.

Ron got up to take one step towards Ty.

"Ty. This might be enough for one day. Here's my card. Sleep on it. Call me, call a friend, call a relative. We all can give you support."

"Yeah, my aunt will talk some sense into her… She's like my second mom."

Pause.

"Ok, I'm gonna leave. 'Bye."

"Good bye, Ty. You will get through this."

Ty looked up and shook his head, then looked down in defeat, heading towards the door.

After leaving Ron's office, Ty decided he wasn't ready to call his parents. He barely made it back to his dorm, the way his head was spinning. He sat on his bottom bunk, staring into space. After an hour had passed, his roommate entered, finding him in that position.

"Hey, man, what's up?" Jake waved his hands in front of Ty's glazed eyes.

Ty swatted his hand away.

"Hey, 'scuse me. Are you tripping or something?"

Ty woke up out of his daze and stood up to look Jake In the face. "Just leave me alone."

"Woah!" Ty's roommate put his hands in the air, "Sorry for lookin' out for ya."

Ty replied in a growl, "If I need your help I'll ask for it". He rose and left the room, slamming the door.

He went out into the night and wandered around campus. A small group of students was sitting on a stone wall when one of them called out, "Ty? You're in my Biology class, right? How's it going?"

Ty tried to ignore her, walking past.

She tried again, "Want some brownies? Seth got a care package and we're stuffing ourselves!"

Ty lost his patience. "Can you just leave me alone?" He hurried past them now, suddenly embarrassed and angry with himself for dumping his anger on her.

A guy in that group stood up and jogged to meet up with Ty. "I think you owe her an apology."

"BACK OFF!" Ty yelled.

For the second time that night a student rose their hands high in surrender to Ty's anger.

"All I can say, dude, is get some help!"

Ty was furious again, tempted to teach that mouthy brat a lesson, but he kept walking without looking back. He couldn't get back to the dorm fast enough. He made a bee line for his bed again, and planned to pretend to be asleep in case his roommate reappeared. Instead, he got a phone call. He saw it was Regina. He was tempted to ignore it. But he answered, and barked, "What?"

"Well, hello, Mr. Sunshine. I'm calling to check on you, and that's what I get?"

"I can't talk right now. I'm too mad."

"About what?"

"I'll tell you sometime later, not now."

"Why not? Now I'm worried."

"Get off my back! I'm hanging up!"

Regina texted him seconds later. *Ty, what's the matter? Is it about your parents?*

He turned off his phone and threw it against the wall. It was going to be a very long night.

The next morning, Ty made it to practice just on time. He was ready early, but wanted to look cool. He had no one to walk with, since he hadn't made any friends yet and his roommate wasn't even remotely interested in sports. At six AM, the humid air had already reached eighty degrees. This was abnormal weather for Maine, with summer approaching its close.

The training was intense, and running in the heat made most of the guys dizzy. Some stopped, bent over, others went off in search of their water bottles. No one had permission to stop the workout. Ty's pace slowed, and he tentatively headed toward the water bottles, but kept jogging in place. His special teams coach approached the buoycotters, taking in a deep breath. "Practice is not optional, men… unless you want to warm the bench all season! The head coach at Alabama is my college buddy… I'm sure he'd be willing to share his field with us, so y'all can get a taste of what hot really means!"

The guys groaned simultaneously and started to run again. Forty minutes later, practice was declared over, and everyone again swarmed toward their water. Ty was searching for the last few drops in his bottle when a teammate bumped his elbow to get his attention. "You a freshman, too? Name's Shawn. I think you're in my dorm."
Ty looked at him. "Yeah, second floor. Ty."
They shook hands.
"You need a workout partner?"
Ty looked confused. "I'm all set, thanks."
Shawn shook his head. "I know you don't have one, and I need a spotter for my lifting."
Ty wasn't sure how to answer. He'd always worked out alone. He supposed things were done differently in college. He decided this might be a chance to make a friend on the team, so he nodded, accepting. "When do you go?"
Shawn looked relieved. "Four o'clock. Every afternoon. Meet me in the weight room. Don't be late," he chuckled.

By the middle of the week Ty was ready to talk to his parents. He texted his father to ask when would be a good time to call. He decided he'd start with his dad because he thought he could get him on his side.
"Hello, Ty, it's good to hear from you," Ty's father said in a warm tone once they connected by phone.
"Dad, Mom's gone off the deep end. Please, tell her to drop this. I don't need a shrink! I worked hard to get into college, now let me enjoy it!"
"Ty, your mom and I are in agreement on this. Please, give Ron a try. We really think you'll come to like him."
"I don't need a friend, and I'm not a project! Stop treating me like a kid!"
"I'm sorry, Ty, we're not wavering on this. Would you like to tell me about school, about the team?"
Ty disconnected the call without a word. He didn't bother to call his mom.

Chapter 2 –September

It was an exceptionally warm afternoon in mid-September. Ron half expected a no-show from Ty. He was pleasantly shocked when the young man walked into the room.

"Hello, Ty. I haven't heard from you at all since we last met, but it's great to see you."

"This is part of the deal, isn't it?"

"Yes, it is. How are you holding up?"

"I'm fine. Really busy with homework and the team."

"Do you mind if I ask how you're adapting to this situation with your parents?"

"Dad won't budge, so I'm not even going to bother to reason with Mom. I'm just holding out until they miss me so much, they'll cave in just to get a call from me. I can beat them at their own game."

Pause.

"My girlfriend's been pretty freaked out about this. It's not just hard on me."

"When did you meet her, recently?"

"No, we've been together since high school. She goes to UNH."

"Is she being supportive to you now?"

"Yeah, but sometimes I just have to hang up because she's slowly starting to take their side. We're spending all our time on the phone arguing; we're not having any fun lately."

"I'm sorry to hear that."

"Yeah, right."

"You doubt my sincerity?" Ron put his hand over his heart. He could see that he and Ty were going to make progress.

A few hours after his therapy session, Ty met up with Shawn in the cafeteria. They pooled their money and bought a pizza in the special junk food line. After they sat down, Shawn proceeded to grill Ty to get to know him. "I never asked you where you're from." "Not far, as you can probably tell by my accent, Augusta. As land locked as you can get in Maine, maybe that's why I took to basketball and baseball as a kid." Shawn shook his head. "Well, I'm a city kid, Boston. This college sure is the back woods for me!" They both laughed. "But, hey, I'm getting to like nature, and a walk in the woods is a great first date! Not that I've had any dates up here yet, but I'm working on it!" Ty decided to ask a few questions of his own. "What did you do for fun in the big city?" "Well, when I was little my dad took me to a lot of Sox games. Then, during high school, me and my crew, we went to concerts and clubs a lot, during the off season. I really loved my varsity football coach, Mr. Grimes. He was old but really cool. Did you like your coaches?" Ty sat in silence for a moment, remembering his high school days as well. "My freshman coach was the best, but the varsity coach was pretty much a jerk. He pushed us, but never gave us any positive feedback. He was always riding us. I suppose that helped me get on this team, but I didn't enjoy my last two years on the high school team." Shawn nodded in understanding.

The new friends chatted for another half hour, then headed back to the dorm. Shawn continued to complain about his lack of a love life, but Ty didn't mind. He was glad to have someone to hang out with in this new environment.

At least four times per week, Shawn and Ty worked out together. One afternoon early in the season, Ty realized he was glad to have a partner to push him and keep him honest. "Coach said I have to focus on my legs… can we start with that?" Ty asked, deferring to Shawn, who seemed so at home in the gym. "You got it, Toyota!" Shawn laughed. They spent the next half hour doing leg presses, squats, and lunges. "It's still light out, let's run the bleachers," Shawn offered. "That's so high school," Ty complained, but he followed his new friend outside for some more sweating.

Chapter 3 – October

It was a crisp, sunny fall afternoon, perfect football weather. All Ty could think of was that night's practice and tomorrow's game… He had even forgotten for a moment that he was sitting in a therapy session. Ron held up four index cards two feet in front of Ty's face, and waved them side to side. That woke him out of his reverie. To Ty, it was like waking up in a cold, lumpy dorm bed instead of a hot tub filled with the beautiful girls of his daydreams.

"Yes…?"

It was a drawn out 'yes', sarcastic and feigning interest.

Ron ignored the attitude and proceeded. "Your parents wrote these four cards as topics of conversation between you and me. They represent important things in your family history. You can pick one card each year, let's say, every fall."

"And…?"

"That's all they said. You're a smart guy, you can figure it out."

"Now YOU sound sarcastic," Ty retorted.

"I'm sorry you can't take a compliment. From what I understand how you were raised, you had ample occasion to do and think for yourself, so why would now be any different?"

Ty nodded his head, wearily. "It seems like I spent my entire life doing chores, earning every damned thing I ever wanted, and my parents never answered any of my questions, they always turned their backs on me and waited for me to answer myself."

"Sounds like they did a good job."

"It wasn't fun, I'll tell you that."

Ty paused as he took a breath.

"All my friends, all the kids on my street, they had NICE parents. Their parents talked to them like NORMAL people. Their parents gave them stuff when they asked for it. I never got SQUAT. I had to earn everything I got."

"Everything?" Ron asked.

"Oh, I'm sorry," Ty answered sarcastically, "Sometimes they gave me used crap."

"Like what?"

"Used clothes from other people, or my mom would steal stuff from the lost and found at the end of summer camp every year."

Ron laughed deeply. "Wow! She sounds creative."

"Go to hell. I can say 'hell', it's in the dictionary."

Ron took that comment in stride. "So, what other swears are in the dictionary... Let's see, I suppose I'll allow 'damn' and 'hell', but no references to excrement, fornication, or donkeys. Ok, time to pick a card."

Ty rolled his eyes and selected the fourth card on his right. His eyes scanned the words on the card.

"This is a f*@!%$*"

"Watch it, Ty." Ron cut him off.

Ty yelled even louder this time. "This is a joke! What is this crap?!"

He got up to pace around. "I've gotta get outta here."

Ron sat calmly. "It's your choice, Ty."

"Don't give me that crap! You know I don't have a goddamn choice!"

Ty sat down. He looked at the card for a long moment. "This is my mom's handwriting. She wrote this."

"Yes."

"I don't know why we're bothering with this therapy crap, she's going to cave."

Silence.

"A few more weeks without a call from me, she's gonna cave."

"What would that look like, Ty, her 'caving in'?"

"She's going to realize this is a stupid plan, it's torturing me, it's not normal, that she needs to go to the nuthouse."

Ty looked at Ron intently. "IS she in the nuthouse?"

"No," Ron calmly replied. "She's out living the high life, as far as I know."

"Doubt it," Ty retorted, his arms crossed.

"That's an interesting thought."

"I mean, she's probably going crazy, missing me, feeling wicked guilty."

"Time will tell. What does that mean on the card, 'Baby, you can do it'? Sounds like a private joke."

Ty sighed. "Back to business, Mr. Business."

"That's my job," Ron replied with a slight smile.

"I'm only going to answer your question because it's part of the deal."

"I'm glad you understand and accept the deal," Ron answered.

"Yahoo."

Ty took a short pause. He stared at the ground as he began again.

"It's a song. My mom always sang corny old songs. Songs I never heard of, stuff they sang in the last century. The dinosaur age."

"Yes," Ron answered, smiling, "the good stuff"

"Whatever," Ty retorted. "I guess I'll give you Led Zeppelin, but that's as far as I'm going."

Ron gave a relaxed smile, then a look that said, 'go on'.

"She always sang these songs when Dad or I said something that she wanted to make a point of; she'd take that word or idea and find a song with those same words. She had a horrible singing voice and she hardly knew any of the words... But it was kind of cool, it was fun."

Ron looked at Ty.

"I used to hassle her about it. I'd say, 'you're embarrassing', or I'd just walk away, rolling my eyes. But I really did like it."

"What's that song all about, the one she wrote on the card? Was it one of her favorites?" Ron asked.

"I don't know. But, she used it the most often, I guess. It was kind of her revenge song... 'Mother knows best' and all that crap. Like, if I did a good job on something, or took something seriously and it came out good, she'd sing it."

Ty exhaled audibly.

"She always made me laugh when she sang that one. Even if I was mad she was right. Like, she almost peed in her pants with joy when I earned money on my own to buy my first bike. I think she thought I was going to give up after the first few bucks."

"What other songs were in her arsenal?"

"'Just Eat It' by Weird Al. You can figure out when she sang that one."

"Touche," said Ron and they both laughed.

Ty looked Ron in the eye. "So, what does this mean? What is she trying to say; you're the psychologist."

"Ty, your mom gave me very little information or direction. She intended for us to navigate this together. Unfortunately for you, my style is not that far from your mom's. I'm here to guide you, but in the end it's up to you to figure things out. There's no perfect answer, no hidden treasure map. You're here to chew on things. Hopefully come up with a different belief about your parents, of your relationship with them, of how they raised you for the past sixteen years."

"Well, Ron, I have no clue, and I have to eat before practice."

"Goodnight, then."

Ty got up to leave. "Bye."

Chapter 4- November

"What is your plan for Thanksgiving break?" Ron inquired.
"MY PLAN?"
Ty gave Ron a scowl.
"Usually, I eat with my family, but they don't give a damn about me anymore, remember?"
Ty stood up and headed to look out the window. He gave the pane a smack with his open palm.
"This is BULLSHIT!"
"Language."
Ty turned to look at Ron.
Ron's eyebrows rose up. "Do you want to apologize?"
Ty ignored Ron's comment and continued. "You know they don't want me for Thanksgiving."
"I doubt that's true. You're refusing to talk to them. Your mom told me she left you several messages inviting you to come home, offering to come pick you up."
Pause.
"Regina and her family are going on to California to be with her grandparents. I wasn't invited. There's loyalty and sympathy at its finest."
"I'm sorry, Ty."
"I'd better be able to catch up on my sleep over break or I'm screwed for finals. It should be quiet in the dorm, since it'll be only me the whole weekend."
Ron waited silently.
"I can't sleep. Hardly at all. Every night it's the same. I fall asleep, weird dreams, then in a couple hours my mind wakes me up, racing. Thinking about what I could do to change their minds, feeling angry, then I get up and walk outside, then come in, and I still can't sleep. Every night. I can't sleep in because of practice and school."

"I know it's no consolation, but it's very normal. When we're feeling hurt or upset, the subconscious mind feels it too, and it tries to sort things out. When we need the rest and healing the most, we often can't get it."

"Well, tell my parents that. This is screwing me up."

"You can tell them yourself, Ty. But for now, let's work on helping you get some sleep. I have an exercise you may want to try. At least try it here so you know how it goes. It's up to you if you choose to use it at the dorm."

Ron moved closer to Ty and positioned his chair so that they are looking at each other directly.

"When you're done with everything you have to do for the day, do one last thing you really enjoy before getting into bed. Not too loud and crazy; maybe listen to a favorite song or write an e mail to a friend. Then, sit on your bed. Close your eyes, straight back and open chest, and breathe in and out; slow, full breaths. Just concentrate on your breathing, in and out. If any thoughts come into your head, gently sweep them away, and focus back on your breathing. Do this for about five minutes, and build up to more time each night. Then, lie down to sleep and try to accept whatever comes, good sleep or restlessness. But I believe this exercise will help calm your mind to help you get a more peaceful sleep."

"That's all yoga crap. I want my problem solved, I'm not interested in accepting it as a 'beautiful part of my life'."

"Ty, I'm not suggesting that you should be happy about what's going in with your parents. But for the time being, you can't change the situation, and your sleep is suffering. When we're faced with unpleasant things that we can't change, we can try to work around them so we don't suffer more than is necessary."

"Ok, I'll try it, but I'm not making any promises."

"That's the spirit!" Ron laughed.

Thanksgiving Day was hard for Ty. He moped around the dorm, eating leftover Chinese takeout and not getting any studying done. He still had not called his parents. He didn't appreciate all the weird looks of shock and sympathy from various students yesterday as they headed out on their holiday with their families. On Friday morning, he went for a long run and was able to study for two hours. He was starting to adjust to this time of solitude. He continued to delete every text and voice mail he received from his parents. Since Wednesday evening, he had counted fourteen.

His ability to sleep had not improved, however, and so when he heard a knocking sound Saturday morning, he assumed it was part of a fuzzy dream. With his pillow cemented over his head, he still could not block out the sound. He decided to get up and check out the noise. He jumped back in surprise as soon as he looked out the window. There was his father, forehead pressed against the glass. Once Ty calmed himself, he just stared at his dad, frozen. Then, his feet decided what to do next. They led him out of the room, rushing to find his parents. Once he opened the building door, he and his dad hugged for a long time. As they drew apart, Ty saw his mother out of the corner of his eye. "I'm pissed at you, but I still want a hug." That was music to his mother's ears, and so she smiled, teary-eyed, and stepped in to get her embrace. Dad broke the ice. "Well, I could eat a bear... what do you say about a big breakfast in town, Ty?"
Ty lifted his head and nodded 'yes'.
They ate in awkward silence, but toward the end of the meal Ty seemed relaxed, so his parents asked him to tell them all about his college experience thus far. He mostly talked about the team and his new friends. When asked if he wanted to go anywhere or do any errands after breakfast, Ty said, "No, thanks, but maybe a walk around campus before you go?"

They took a long walk, with Ty as tour guide, his spirits lifting as they went along. After the tour, they followed him into his dorm for their goodbyes. His reality came rushing back to him, and Ty broached the subject again. "Why do you have to control me with the stupid therapy thing? I'm not a kid, and I don't have any problems, so stop treating me like some special ed kid!" He was feeling heated now.

Ty's mother took a deep breath and looked directly at Ty. "This is our last chance to help you with the hurt and anger you are carrying. After college, you are a completely free agent, on your own, supporting yourself. The many times we tried therapy when you were in school, you refused to cooperate, to accept the help."

Ty looked livid, and his father stepped in. "I see we're not going to solve this today. Can we give it more time?"

"You're not the one who has to go to therapy, Dad," Ty retorted. "I want this solved now."

His parents looked at each other, then his father said, "Well, Ty, we're going to head out. We don't want to continue the argument. Please call us any time, or come home any time."

"Am I 'allowed' to come home even if I refuse to cooperate with your stupid plan?"

His mother looked at him, her eyes soft. "Of course, Ty, and I'd be happy to come pick you up, you just say the word."

Ty just shook his head and lead them out to the parking lot, keeping his distance to avoid any parting hugs.

Chapter 5- December

Ty flopped down into the chair facing Ron. He did not look happy to be there.

"Why so glum?"

"Would you like MY life?" Ty retorted.

Ron laughed.

"What about counting your blessings? Let's start with me... I'm healthy, I have a lot of love in my life, I have a successful career, I had an excellent lunch..."

Ron looked at Ty, encouraging him to do the same.

Ty rolled his eyes and got up to look out the window.

"Regina is really getting on my nerves. It's the same old story every time, she thinks I'm not spending enough time with her. She's got her own friends at her campus, why can't she spend some weekends with them instead of always coming here?"

"Maybe her cafeteria food stinks."

"Ha ha. We never used to fight. It's not fun anymore, being around her."

"What do you think has changed?"

"She can't see me every day to keep tabs on me. I think that drives her crazy, and its really ticking me off, the constant nagging."

"It couldn't possibly be that she misses you?"

"Doubt it. Like I said, all we do is fight. In person, on the phone."

"You said you never used to fight..."

"Yeah, she was my rock, she calmed me down, and we used to have a lot of fun."

"Why would you need to calm down?"

"My parents were always on my back... Specifically, my mother."

"And now...?"

Ty took a deep breath.

"Are you saying what I think you're saying, you head shrink?"

"Probably. What am I saying?"

"That since I'm trying to limit my contact with my parents, I fight with Regina as a substitute."

Ron's eyes softened and he exhaled. Ron was impressed with Ty's insight.

"So, are you two on a break or something?"

"I don't know. We don't really talk about it."

Ty decided to go home for Christmas. He figured he could survive his parents for about five days, spending the bulk of it catching up with his high school friends. There were several relatives at Christmas dinner, and Ty dodged any attempts his parents made at a discussion about his therapy. By the fourth day, it was apparent they all finally decided to put the difficult topic on ice and just enjoy each other's company. Overall, it was a relaxing time and he got along with his parents and had a few nice moments with them, usually while cooking or washing the dishes together. At the end of his visit, his father drove him back to school, and agreed to shoot some baskets in the gym before leaving. Ty gave him a hug before he left.

"Thank you for coming home for Christmas, Ty, it meant the world to your mom and me."

"It was ok, I'm glad I did."

"We'll get through this, Ty. Please know we are doing this out of love. We love you very much."

Ty decided to bite his tongue. "Have a safe trip, Dad."

His father nodded and returned to his car.

Chapter 6 - January

"So, how was your holiday? Did you see Regina over the break?" Ron inquired.
"It was pretty good. But we broke up."
"Oh?"
"I tried first in person, New Year's Eve, but she started crying. Then, the next night, she called me and said, 'Ok, I'm ready.'"
"How do you feel about it?"
"I'm glad it was mutual. Less drama that way. We don't talk any more on the phone but we text a little about school and stuff, nothing too personal. I miss her sometimes, but I'm so busy. She's better off with someone who can do more stuff with her."
Ron nodded slightly. "Would you believe me if I say it's good that you miss her?"
"One of my goals is to get over that feeling," Ty retorted.
"But at least you're feeling the loss. To heal, we need to feel the pain and then let it go."
"There you go again, 'Let it go, like a kite flowing across the ocean, like a ray of sunshine over the treetops.'" Ty made a dramatic gesture with his arms outstretched, swaying above his head.
Ron laughed. "Can I use your material with my other clients? That's good stuff!"
They both laughed.
"Well, since you're officially a free man, what do you say you cream me at some hoops and then I buy you a burger?"
"I wouldn't be caught dead with my shrink out on campus!"
"I belong to the Y, OFF campus, and if you run into anyone you know, you can pretend you don't know me."
"Alright. But you better not have heart trouble, old man, 'cause I'm going to bring you DOWN!"
They both laughed again.

The sun had just set, and it was odd weather for January in Maine… drizzle, fog, and forty seven degrees. Within the last two minutes of the game, Ty was called off the bench as they formed a huddle. The Black Bears were at their opponent's twenty-five yard line. The head coach was about to announce the strategy to use these last two minutes to seal the win.

Ty's heart was pounding in his chest, the crowd was loud and animated. He barely caught all the details of the play. This was his big chance to show what he was made of. A great opportunity for a freshman running back. He knew where his parents were sitting in the stands, but he decided not to look at them; he needed to focus.

As the center snapped the ball to the quarterback, Ty ran toward the line of scrimmage. His friend, Shawn, as full back, started to implement his part of the play, to open up a gap in the front line so Ty could pass through and run the ball.

Ty ran toward the right, where he was expecting Shawn to open the line for him. Shawn went left, however, and Ty was tackled. The play was over. Ty got up, shook his head clear, and looked frantically around for Shawn. He found him walking toward the bench. Without a word, Ty shoved him from behind. "What's your problem?" Shawn yelled, whirling around.

"You screwed up the play! That was my chance for a TD, you asshole!" Ty yelled, breathless. Shawn was angry, but he could see Ty's point; he'd feel the same way if that happened to him. "I'm sorry, man. I thought I heard Coach say 'right', not 'left'." Ty walked away from him without an answer. He was still fuming.

Once inside the locker room, the head coach called out Ty's and Shawn's names. They followed him into his office, closing the door behind them. Ty started to open his mouth to yell more indignations when the coach stopped him with an open palm in the air. "I believe I'm the coach, so I get the first word. Shawn, you screwed up the play. But that's not a federal offense, especially when we were four touchdowns ahead with only two minutes left." Ty looked down, breathing heavily, trying to control himself. "Mr. Running Back, on the other hand, has behaved badly. Not only did you try to pick a physical fight with Shawn, you did it in front of the television camera and a stadium full of fans."

Ty did not reply. He kept his eyes averted. "I thought you two were friends." "We are," Shawn answered for the both of them. Ty looked up, surprised. "I'm sorry, Shawn. I just lost it. I know you didn't mean to rob me of the TD. It was really loud out there." Both boys physically relaxed. The coach, on the other hand, was still worked up. "If you so much as touch a player in anger again, you will be benched for several games. Ty, you need to work on your self-control. You can't act on every impulse, because if you do, you will be kicked off this team." Ty nodded, his eyes down. "You're getting a reprimand in your file. I expect perfect behavior if you want to be considered for any plays in the championship game next week." "Yes, sir," Ty said in a low voice. "You're both dismissed." the coach said, as he got up from his desk.

Close to midnight, four of the players, along with Ty and Shawn, headed back to their dorm. Ty hung back as they entered the building. He was grateful to see Shawn do the same.

Ty started to speak, "I'm…"

Shawn cut him off. "Stay out of my face for a while. When I'm ready to hear your apology, I'll find you."

Ty nodded and headed for his dorm without a word. He saw his parents had sent him a text message, but he decided to turn off his phone and attempt to get some sleep.

Three days later, Ty approached Shawn at his usual spot in the library. "You still need help on your Algebra?"
Shawn rose to his feet and answered in a quiet voice as he looked squarely at Ty. "I asked you to give me some space."
Ty looked at his feet. "I know, but you said you had a big test on Friday."
Shawn sat down and sighed. "Okay, man, I guess so. I really need some help." He gestured for Ty to sit next to him. "I just want you to know, I think you have a major anger problem and you should do something about it before it ruins your life."
Ty exhaled. "My parents are already forcing me to see a shrink, isn't that enough?"
"Just don't stop going, 'cause you obviously still have more work to do."
Ty gave him an offended look.
"You know what I'm talking about. Like, when you used to yell and scream at poor Regina all the time. Dude, that's not cool. She's the sweetest girl, and her only crime was she wanted to spend more time with you!" Shawn shook his head in sad disbelief.
"Okay, I get it," Ty replied in a defeated tone. "Now, can you take out your Math book already?"
The two set to work.

Chapter 7 - February

Ron was trying to warm himself with a cup of hot green tea when Ty came in for his session.

"Could it be any colder?!!" Ty exclaimed.

"Are you from Florida?"

"No, but damn, it's cold!"

They both laughed.

"Hey, you got any hot stuff for me?"

"You know where the machine is." Ron shook his head and smiled.

Ty went back to the reception area to get a hot chocolate from the dispenser. As he came back in, he seemed relaxed.

"You strike me as being in a good mood today, Ty... Any particular reason?"

"Well, since you asked, I guess I'm starting to enjoy bachelorhood again. Me and my buds are having fun on the weekends again. We can do whatever we want. My new rule is I don't party with couples, only free agents who won't kill my buzz with what their girlfriends want or don't want to do that night. I'm so done with that!"

Ron laughed. "Well, enjoy it while you can. You never know when you will be struck by Cupid's arrow again."

Ty shook his head. "Not for a long time, if I can help it. I'm finally a free man, I can enjoy the TRUE college experience!"

"Does that involve vomiting, by chance?"

Ty laughed. "Sometimes."

"Wow, I miss my college days of partying, puking, and other regrettable acts... NOT!" Ron was enjoying their banter, but it was time to get to work, so he sat up straighter and put his cup aside.

"So, are you keeping your nose clean in the anger management department?"

Ty bristled at the comment. "I'm still on the team, if that answers your question."

"I'm glad, Ty."

"Shawn and I are still good friends, you know. It blew over, and no, I haven't chosen any new victims."

"Superb. Enjoy your friendships, and lean on your friends. Can you do that, Ty, talk to your friends about things that bother you or make you angry?"

Ty stretched out his legs. "Maybe with Shawn. He's cool."

"Does he know about the situation with your parents?" Ron inquired.

"The bare minimum. Hey, I don't need to spill my guts to him when I'm forced to do it with you."

Ron leaned in and looked at Ty squarely in the face. "What would you say makes Shawn such a good friend?"

"We have a lot of fun together."

"What else? We're just getting started," said Ron.

"I respect him, on and off the field. He's the real deal."

"Does he ever seem to have any struggles in life, and does he ever talk about them?"

"His parents are wrapping up a nasty divorce. He talks about it a lot."

"Do you think talking about it helps him cope?"

"I don't know," Ty replied.

Ron smiled. "You and Shawn are probably feeling very similar things. I know you say you're not comfortable with sharing your personal information with your friends, but maybe you would consider, at the very least, letting Shawn in on more of the details of your situation. You may be surprised how much better you feel just knowing that someone can relate. I believe he will be able to understand on some level."

"We'll see," said Ty. "I'll play it by ear. I'm not going to start some sort of therapy session talk with him, it'll have to come up naturally."

"I hope you will consider trying it out, Ty. You need more people in your corner than just me."

Ty smiled a bit. "You know, you're right. I don't want to be dependent on you for the rest of my life. Believe me, come graduation, you'll never see me again!"

Ron laughed, then extended his hand out to Ty for a shake, signaling it was the end of their session.

The following Saturday afternoon, Ty and Shawn set off across the campus green to the gym building for their daily workout together. As usual, Shawn updated Ty on the divorce.

"At least I've learned to do one thing, Ty. Now, when I get the sense that one of my parents is going to start talking negative, that's when I say I have to go, and I end the phone call. My life has been amazingly more peaceful!"

They both laughed.

As Ty came to a dead stop, Shawn noticed and turned around to face him. "Did you forget your lifting gloves again?"

Ty paused, then answered, "No. I just wanted to ask you, how come you tell me all about the crap going on in your family. Aren't you embarrassed?"

Shawn didn't know how to answer at first. He couldn't figure out if Ty was being judgmental or not. "What do you mean, you're sick of my venting?"

"No, Shawn, seriously, you can tell me anything. I just don't know why you trust me, telling me all the crazy stuff in your life."

Shawn laughed slightly. "You have crazy shit, too, ya know."

"That's exactly why I'm asking you," Ty answered.

"So, then why are we having this conversation?" Shawn asked.

Ty started walking and Shawn followed suit.

"I'm asking you why you trust me to not think you're as crazy as your parents. Why you trust me not to spread your personal business all over the team, or all over campus," Ty asked.

Shawn laughed hard now, then answered seriously. "'Cause I know you have my back."
"Just like that?" asked Ty.
"Well, it was a little dicey a few weeks back, if you know what I mean, but we worked it out and you're someone I know I can count on. I know what kind of person you are, Ty. You're not that hard to read. Loyalty is in your DNA."
Ty shook his head. It was swimming.
"Alright, already, Ty. I know some crazy stuff is going down with *your* family and you want to get it off your chest."
"I don't know. I guess I just want you to be in my corner. One hundred percent."
"Then, tell me what's going on. All I get is bits and pieces that you accidentally let slip out. When I ask you directly, you clam up."
"Ok, I will. Thanks, Shawn."
Shawn answered with a radio announcer's voice, "To be continued!"
"Stop embarrassing me, freak," answered Ty.
Shawn punched Ty's arm in a friendly way and they entered the building.

Chapter 8: MARCH

Shawn counted the reps as Ty pushed himself at the bench press. They were both glad to be wrapping up this grueling workout. They worked particularly hard today, and were exhausted. As they headed to the locker room, Shawn changed course to approach an older man sitting in a wheelchair. With his bulging biceps and crewcut, he looked like a Marine; probably injured in Afghanistan or Iraq. Ty passed them, hoping to make a beeline to the showers, when Shawn caught his arm. "Hey, I want you to meet my workout partner, Ty; he's a running back." Shawn said to the man, who then extended a strong hand to Ty. As they shook hands, Ty couldn't help but feel awkward, so he averted his eyes. "I'm Mac. You can look at my legs; it's okay. I'm even used to kids poking at them to see if they move!" Mac and Shawn chuckled. Ty looked at Mac and said, "Good to meet you, Mac." He was still nervous. Shawn interrupted, "Hey, you need a partner for your workout today?" Mac nodded and replied, "Yeah, my usual guy had a test so I was going to scale down my workout, but if you're offering..." Shawn smiled and turned to Ty, "You're free now, aren't you, Ty? All you need to do is pull down the high overhead bars so Mac can reach them, and he'll do all the rest. Twenty minutes tops, right, Mac?" Ty was feeling very hot in the face. This was way out of his comfort zone, but he was too shy to say 'no', so he just nodded. "Ok," Mac said, "looks like I'll get a real workout after all. See you later, Shawn." Shawn punched Ty's arm to indicate to him that it would be fine, then left quickly, not giving Ty a chance to change his mind.

Ty stood, frozen and silent. Mac had his work cut out for him. "Ok, so you're not used to this sort of thing. Let's break the ice first. Do you want to know why I'm a paraplegic?" Ty nodded. "I took a bad fall in an explosion in Baghdad. Army police." Ty nodded again. He decided to relax a bit. "Why do your legs look kind of… muscular?" Mac smiled. "That's top secret… Let's just say I have 'people'." Ty smiled and nodded. "Let's get to work so you can get outta here," Mac offered.

Ty followed all of Mac's instructions for the next twenty five minutes and was amazed at what Mac was capable of. He completely worked out his arms and his core, and his strength was impressive. He pushed himself, but within safe and healthy limits. 'I would kill for biceps like that', he thought. "So," Mac interrupted Ty's thoughts, "you ever go to a Rugby game?" Ty answered in the negative. "But that would be cool. You want me to watch a game with you?" Mac smiled, "Actually, I'm *in* the game. Captain of the team this year. We play every Saturday night; Shawn knows the venue. You'd have a great time." Ty was amazed. He nodded, speechless again. "We'll try to go to one of your games soon." They shook hands and Ty left the gym. He still felt nervous, but he realized that he was glad he met Mac today.

The following Friday, Ty went to the student lounge where he bought a pizza and settled down to attempt some studying. Just as he was getting in the groove, he felt a tap on his shoulder. "Hey, you, aren't you Ty?" A young woman whose face was familiar to Ty sat down on the bench next to him. "Oh, hi, aren't you in my Physiology class?" "Yeah, I'm Lisa." She smiled and put her backpack down, apparently inviting herself to join him. She extended her hand, Ty shook it, then he sheepishly offered her some of his now cold pizza. "Thanks, but I'm all set, my roommate is waiting for me outside. We're getting ready to go see a live band tonight, you interested?" Ty blushed, took a breath, then nodded. He cleared his throat. "Yeah, that would be cool. Where should I meet you?" Lisa gave him the information and she waved goodbye. Ty tried to get in another half hour of work, but he couldn't concentrate. Lisa was cute, and he was flattered she invited him out.

He went back to the dorm and showered, shaved, then paced the room until it was time to leave.

He found Lisa and her small group of friends standing by a blue SUV. They made their introductions and headed out to the bar. The evening went well; Ty liked the music and he was relieved he didn't have to make small talk all night. Lisa smiled at him a few times, and attempted light hearted conversation a few times over the loud noise. When they were delivered back to their original meeting spot back on campus, Ty lingered, wondering if Lisa would want him to walk her back to her dorm. Luckily, she picked up on his cue. "Hey, Ty, you want to walk me back to my room?" Ty nodded. He asked her where she was from, what her major was, and he felt comfortable with her. He was very attracted to her, wondering why he hadn't really noticed her before now.

When they arrived at her building, she invited him in. Her room was a single, and when they entered, Ty wondered what her intentions were. He wasn't opposed to the idea of staying the night, but he didn't really know her that well, so he wasn't sure what he wanted. Lisa apparently knew what she wanted. "Have a seat." She gestured toward the bed, since there was only one chair in the room. She sat next to him, they talked some more, then she turned to him for a kiss. Being with a woman felt good; Ty had missed it. He decided to go with the flow. They kissed for a long while more, and Ty still had not made a move. Lisa broke the ice. "I'd like to do a little more than, you know, kiss." She started to massage his shoulders. She kissed his neck. Ty began to feel uncomfortable. She was taking the lead, and he just couldn't bring himself to be aggressive. He hardly knew her; it felt weird. The only other woman he had been with was Regina, and they had taken it slow. They didn't start making love until the summer after graduation. He forced himself out of his reverie and told himself to stop thinking and just enjoy it. He tried to return her advances, and it felt alright for a while, but he kept thinking, 'this is a stranger'. He just wasn't into it.

Lisa finally picked up on this, and said to Ty, "What's the matter? Do you need a drink or something to loosen you up? Sorry, I don't have anything... being under age and all..." Ty blushed again. "No, hey, I'm sorry, I'm just not in the mood. I'm totally over my old girlfriend, but I feel, kind of guilty." Lisa nodded. "I understand. It's too soon, that's all." She exhaled, looked a bit defeated, then put on a smile. "No hard feelings. Maybe some other time."

Ty smiled weakly. "Yeah, maybe some other time."

On his short walk back to his room, he beat himself up mentally for the wasted opportunity. 'I must be going crazy,' he thought to himself.

Chapter 9: APRIL

Ron paced in his office, putting the final touches on his plans for this month's session with Ty. He was comfortably seated when Ty barged in, five minutes late.

"Well, hello, stranger."

"Hey, Ron, sorry I'm late, I totally forgot about today."

"At least you made it. We can stay thirty minutes extra to atone." Ron said with mock seriousness.

"Very funny. I said I was sorry. You're lucky I even come to these meetings!"

Ron took a deep breath. He was getting attitude and they were only seconds into the session.

"So, how does it feel to be done with your season?"

"Actually, I miss the routine, and of course the games, but I was so tired near the end, I'm glad it's over. I can actually party now!"

Ron laughed. "Not too hard, I hope. I want to ask you how it's going between you and your parents."

"Funny you should ask... I'm pissed at them. Not just for this stupid forced counseling, but because they want me to live at home this summer. Work for my mom's company as a stupid messenger boy."

Ron offered, "Would they give you permission to live up here if you found a job, paid your own expenses?"

"I don't know. I didn't ask. They just want to control me! First counseling, now prison!"

"Wait a minute, you're jumping to conclusions. Why don't you ask them?"

"I don't see why they can't pay a few extra months on my dorm so I can get a job up here this summer."

"Wait a minute, you want your freedom, but on your parents' dime?"

"It's not like I wouldn't be working, I'd get a full-time job!" Ty was getting annoyed.

"Ty, I think I have to side with your parents on this one… Why should they pay for your living expenses this summer when you can stay back at your house at no cost to them?" Ty stood up and rubbed his face in frustration. "You're just like them! You don't care about me, just about rules and conditions!"

"Well, Ty, you can fix this situation very easily… earn enough money to pay your own way this summer."

"Are we almost done? I'm getting really angry."

Ron waited a moment before speaking. "When a child becomes an adult, they naturally want freedom. But freedom comes with responsibility, and independence is not free. Does anyone pay your parents' living expenses?"

"Of course not!" Ty was exasperated.

"Why don't you let that sink in for a bit. Yes, we can end early today. But I will ask you to go take a run or shoot some hoops or hang out with a friend, to dissipate this anger you've built up today. Bad on your ticker and your nerves!" Ron chided, warmly.

Ty and Shawn convinced their teammate, Markie, to drive them to Mac's Rugby game on a rainy Saturday night. "I don't know if I wanna watch a bunch of handicapped vets play ball!" Markie said, uncomfortably. "I can pick you guys up when it's over." Shawn would have none of it. "Give us ten minutes and I guarantee you'll be begging to stay. The way Mac described it, it's full-throttle mortal combat. Hell, half the guys on the team competed in the Paralympics last year in London, and a few of them compete in the World Championships… Nothing depressing about it!" Markie looked at Ty, who just smiled and shrugged his shoulders.

When they entered the gymnasium, Ty was surprised to see so many people in attendance. On one side, most of the spectators wore blue shirts, and on the other, he saw a sea of red shirts, all emblazoned with the words, "Quad Rugby USA". 'These are hard-core fans', he thought to himself. The playing area looked like a basketball court, and there was a goal area on each end. A volleyball was used to allow for easier grip, especially for the players with little or no use of their hands.

After they settled in on the bleachers, Mac's team came out in blue jerseys, and started to warm up. They weren't in regular motorized wheelchairs; instead, everyone was outfitted in custom manual chairs that looked like tanks. They had huge hubcap type things on each side, angled-in to shield the wheels, and a low cage-type bar in front that looked like a bumper. The players appeared like soldiers in suits of armor. Ty's buddies were bug-eyed over the contraptions as well. Ty stole some glances at the players. Most were as muscular as Mac, and several were covered in tattoos. Some of the guys were missing their arms, at the forearm or upper arm. Nonetheless, they pushed the wheels of their chairs with what they had left of their appendages. In short order, Ty could no longer see these physical traits; the power and performance of these athletes took up all his attention.

Ty turned his head sharply in the direction of a loud banging sound, to see two teammates actually going at it like battering rams. They crashed into each other over and over, then would take a break to have a discussion, apparently over technique. At last, the red team took their turn to warm up on the court, and then the game began. With four players on each side, it was chaos and excitement. Possession of the ball changed sides often and at an extremely fast pace. Left and right, players were clashing, many falling backward on the floor, still securely in their chairs. The most points, five, were awarded for bringing the ball into the goal area, called a try. With three defenders in the goal area, most goals were blocked, usually via strikes and holds. A strike served to bump into the opponent's chair, and a hold was used to prevent them from advancing. Mac spent a fair amount of time yelling out instructions to the players, and Ty had to laugh when the apparently more seasoned players ignored their captain and forged ahead on their own steam. Nonetheless, the blue team appeared to be having fun and working together well.

All eyes were riveted on the game the entire time, and the level of testosterone in the room was at its bursting point. Each player looked determined, fierce, talented, and the exact opposite of 'disabled'. They were so alive, the feeling was contagious. Ty understood immediately why so many dedicated fans followed these teams. He felt very proud of Mac, and very happy to know that these men had an arena where they could feel powerful and athletic again. Ty was simply blown away. All his stereotypes were crushed forever. The red team triumphed, with a final score of 75 to 69. Mac's team took it well and gave hearty congratulations to their opponents and friends.

Chapter 10: MAY

Over Memorial Day weekend, Ty took the bus home to visit his parents. A few of his high school friends were going home as well, so he was looking forward to it. On the second morning at home, his dad caught him in the kitchen. "Hey, Ty, you want to shoot some hoops or take Lacy for a run tonight?"

"Sure, dad, if we can be done by eight, I'm meeting up with my friends at nine."

"No problem, let's head out around six and grab a bite after. Mom's going to Grandma's for supper tonight so we're on our own."

Later that morning, Ty took Lacy for a long walk past his old haunts. So many good memories, he realized. All the games, the good times with Regina, the pranks he and his buddies pulled over the years, all harmless. After a lunch of cold cereal back at the house, he found himself going through the box of momentos in his bedroom. His yearbooks, filled with signatures from his friends and teachers, held his attention for an hour. He then eyed a photo album. When he opened it, he realized immediately what it was. He hadn't looked at it since he was in elementary school. It was sparse, but told a story. The album contained his baby pictures and other documents from the time he lived with his birth mother. Some of the photos were ripped, but they were glued and taped back together, all carefully preserved and arranged lovingly in the album. His adoptive mom had also inserted pastel colored cardstock rectangles here and there with details about his life that she wrote, pieced together from what the social workers had told her. "Ty walked at eleven months." "Ty had many ear infections." "Ty loved broccoli and orange soda." "Ty loved to dance, as soon as he could stand up!" Ty was surprised by these notes. His mom went to all that trouble. He suddenly felt uncomfortable, and he shut the album and slid the box under his bed. He went outside to get some air. He stared into space for a long while, waiting for his father to come home.

After Ty and his father finished their run with the dog, they headed over to an Italian restaurant, Ty's favorite. They rarely ate Italian as a family, his mom disliking most carbs. He felt this was something he and his dad shared exclusively, and he savored every bite and enjoyed their time together.

"So, what did you do today?" his father asked, casually.

"Do I have to report my activities, Sargeant?"

His father was surprised at the rebuke. "No, I was just showing an interest. You don't have to answer the question, you're not on trial."

Ty paused, then had a change of heart. "I dug out the box of albums from under my bed. I found the one with my baby pictures."

"Do you mean when you were an infant, before you came to live with us?"

"Yeah. How did Mom get her hands on all those photos, and the information she wrote down, like what kind of food I liked as a baby?"

His father smiled, then laughed. "That's your mom... dedicated as a bloodhound! She felt it was important, so she did what it took to get them... Let's say I was impressed by her tactics and her efforts. She made endless calls, knocked on neighbors' doors where you used to live, talked to umpteen social workers, and, by god, she got the goods!"

They both laughed.

Ty's father continued. "You know that you mean the world to us, Ty, don't you?"

An awkward silence filled the space for a moment, and both father and son stared into their plates.

Ty took a deep inhale. "Yeah, I do. It's just sometimes it doesn't feel like it. When you set up all these rules, it's like you're daring me to get lost."

"Wow, I had no idea you felt that way. I'm really sorry. We love you more than anything in the world. Maybe too much! I hope someday soon you'll come to understand that. Everything we do regarding you is thoughtful, loving, and with your future in mind. Raising a child is a very big responsibility, and we take it seriously."

"Why can't you guys just let loose once in a while!"

"We're trying, Ty. You have a little ways to go yet, but you're slowly becoming a responsible young adult."

"Well, I hope I can convince you guys soon, because you're cramping my style!"

They both laughed and finished up their delicious meals.

Chapter 11 June

Ty bounced into Ron's office and flopped down in a chair. "I'm in a good mood, so don't spoil it."

"Well, hello to you, too. I'm doing well, thank you for asking." Ron retorted, shaking his head.

"Sorry, but I'm serious. I got a killer summer job… Running the alpine slides at Snowshoe Mountain. Half my dorm is gonna work there… lots of partying every night!"

"Woah, partner. Sounds like you're going to drink your paychecks away."

"I'll be careful, 'Mom'. I told you not to kill my buzz!" They both laughed.

"Well, I'm happy for you, Ty. Sounds like a fun summer ahead. What's that, about thirty minutes away from here? You will be able to come to our sessions without any trouble."

"Oh, joy!"

"And, drumroll, please, you don't have to live at home!"

"About that", Ty spoke hesitantly, "you were right. I was really a tool thinking I had the right to demand that my parents finance my summer expenses on my terms."

Ron smiled. "Wow, I am very happy to hear that. So, how did your semester wrap up? I trust you learned something this year?"

"I passed every class. No summer school for me, buddy!"

"Glad to hear it."

On the last day of June, Ty took the bus with two of his teammates over to the resort to begin their summer job. The park was a grassy valley, surrounded by pines and a large hill. In winter, the hill was used for snow tubing; in summer, it offered an alpine slide and zip lines. The slide looked too tame for Ty's taste, but the zip lines looked fun, and he hoped he would be assigned to those. The new hires spent the day learning how to use and operate the equipment safely, and how to handle difficult customers. Ty's first aid experience was what landed him this job, and so he helped out with the training, gravitating towards the young women who asked for his help to wrap an ace bandage or where to place an ice pack. After dinner in the staff cafeteria, Ty joined a large group of trainees who headed over to China Lake for a swim. Most of the guys did cannonballs off a dock, and showed off for the girls. Ty was a bit jealous of the few guys who had their girlfriends present, splashing and kissing in the water. He joined his teammates in a few races, crawl stroke being his specialty; he won two out five.

He bunked with two teammates and a third guy from another school, and they all seemed to get along well. They spent their first night sampling each other's favorite music and texting on their phones. Ty felt comfortable and happy to have this setup.

Chapter 12 July

After a ten day heat wave, the early evening was cool and refreshing. As Ty sat down to face Ron, he lowered his head to remove his Red Sox hat.

"Evening, Ty. I'm glad to see you made it; that must mean you've managed to evade the police thus far despite your underage drinking."

"Don't you know it. Hey, why do you always assume the worst?"

"Hmmm... let's see, I believe you spelled out to me in great detail your partying plans for the summer."

As Ty straightened up, Ron took in a sharp breath.

"A shiner."

"Yes, Ron, it's none of your business."

"Okay."

Ron kept staring at Ty's black eye.

"Stop staring. It's rude to stare."

"Can't help it."

"Just so you know, I didn't start it."

Ron nodded his head, silent.

"I'm serious. Some jerkface from Bates didn't like me putting the moves on his woman. They didn't even act like a couple, so how the hell was I supposed to know?"

Pause.

"He started dissing me, saying that I'm just a dumb jock whose days at college are numbered. That I probably get a free pass to fail every course because they need me on the team."

"Well, Ty, you had a choice."

"Yeah, yeah, to walk away? NO WAY."

"Are you sure the boy or his family aren't going to press charges?"

"Wait a minute, don't you see MY EYE?"

Silence.

"I knocked him to the ground. When he got up, he started walking away like it was no big deal, and then he turned around and sucker punched me. So, I don't see how any of it's my fault."

"Interesting line of thinking."

"Bite me. Self defense, Ron."

"He teased you, Ty. Why did you take the bait?"

"Yes, yes, I know, itching for a fight. So turn me in already."

"So, what happened, did either of you get fired?"

"No, we both kept our mouths shut. Now I ignore him; I don't hang out with his stupid clique at night. I've got lots of other friends there."

"That's a good first step. Glad to hear it."

"You don't have to believe me, but I swear I was never in a fight IN MY LIFE before this. A physical fight, I mean."

"I believe you."

Pause.

"I see that the bruise is toward the outer edge of your eye."

"Yeah, it's not like we were facing each other head on or anything. It came out of the blue."

"Well, another inch away from your eye and you might be dead now."

"What the hell are you talking about, Drama King?"

"I'm not kidding, Ty."

Ron pointed to the side of his head.

"What do you call this body part?"

"I don't know, the temple, I guess."

"Exactly. If you don't believe me, look it up."

Pause.

"In light of all this, I have an assignment for you. For the next month, I need you to do a punching bag workout for thirty minutes, at least four times a week. Do they have a gym at your resort?"

"Homework?!?"

Pause.

"They do have a gym, but it's not gonna work out. No way."

Pause.

"It's only open to staff between five and seven... AM!"

"That's perfect! It will give you time to shower and eat before your shift starts."

"Ok, I'll tell you I'm going to do it, but that's between me and the punching bag."

Ron smiled like the Mona Lisa. "Not exactly. I'll need proof. Send me a picture from your phone at the start of every session and another once you've completed the thirty minutes. Believe me, I'll know from your face if you did the homework or not."

"I can just spray myself with water and pretend it's sweat." Ron laughed.

"I mean your facial expression. It will look like night and day, the before and after photos. My doctoral thesis was actually on line-up photos. I've 'done' a LOT of prison time, and believe me, faces do not lie."

They both laughed.

"That's pretty cool," Ty admitted.

"Ok, that wraps up this enjoyable session. For next month, reserve a workout room on campus and I'll meet you there instead of here at the office."

SOPHOMORE YEAR

Chapter 13 August

Ron entered the athletic building on campus and was shown to the reserved workout room. It was still dark, so Ron turned on the lights and assessed the room. "Good man." he thought to himself. There was in fact a punching bag in the room, along with other equipment.

Ron did not have long to wait. Ty strutted in, wearing his workout clothing, then started hopping around like a boxer, throwing swings into the air.

"This should be a fun session." laughed Ron.

"Ron, you're gonna bust a gut."

"What?"

"The guy who gave me a shiner… we were stuck working the same ride for a solid WEEK. We had to stand, like, one yard apart the WHOLE TIME."

Ron raised an eyebrow.

"After about an hour, we must have called a truce because we started talking and kind of got to know each other. He works out with me in the mornings now."

Ron laughed with delight.

"So, he hasn't hassled you for sending photos to your therapist?"

"Oh, young innocent, I've got that covered. I just told him it was for my special teams coach, and he ate it right up. He's my photographer now!"

They both laughed.

"So, are you ready to be impressed?"

"Of course! I've only seen the before and after, we're here to show me the middle."

They laughed again.

"Just one thing before you begin, Champ. I'm asking you to ponder one thing. It's a yes or no question, no room for MAYBE's. And I don't want the answer, I want you to just think about it. For the sixteen years you lived at home, did you use your mom as your anger outlet, your punching bag?"

Ty's shoulders raised and tightened. His eyes went dark. He didn't say a word.

Ron did not outwardly react to Ty's sour mood. He brightened his voice to say, "Ok, Ty, show me your stuff." Then, he sat down, rifled through his briefcase, and pulled out his favorite magazine.

As Ty walked into Ron's office, he was greeted enthusiastically.

"Hey, it's Mohammed Ali."

"No doubt, I am WAY BUFF with all those workouts this summer! Team practice is a breeze now. Some of the guys who just partied all summer are wicked jealous."

Ron smiled widely. "I'm glad you got something out of your homework. So, now onto the serious stuff."

Ty tipped his head back and took a deep breath. "When is it ever easy with you?"

"Glad you understand and appreciate my role here. Let's get started. When you broke up with your girlfriend, you told me you two never used to fight."

"Yeah, not until we started at college."

"What might you attribute that to?"

"How about, the extreme stress of my parents threatening to cut me off?"

"That's part of it. Anything else?"

"I was under a lot of pressure, just like I already went through with you the last time we covered this topic."

"I'd like to ask you to leave room for another layer of truth. Let's go back to before the fights with your girlfriend. Are you telling me you two never fought back in high school?"

"Nope."

"Do you remember the question I asked you to mull over as you did the workout last month?"

"Yeah." Ty took another deep breath.

"Did you give it some thought, did you commit to a yes or a no?"

Ty stood up.

"When we were in the gym you said I didn't have to answer it. I did the thinking, now can't you just leave me alone? Can't I have any privacy at all?"

"Ty, I believe that you did the work. Now I need to hear you say it."

"Maybe I don't have to answer every goddamned question you throw at me."

Long pause. Ty slowly walked to the window and stared onto the green grass below.

"Yes, she was my punching bag. Are you happy now?"

"Thank you, Ty. I appreciate you trusting me enough to share that. Would you sit down so we can continue, please?"

Ty hesitated, then sat down.

"What happened to your proverbial punching bag when you came to college?"

"My mother wasn't there any more to take out my frustrations on."

"Exactly. Let's continue a bit more down the path of your freshman year. When did you and your teammate friend have the fight over the missed play?"

"After Regina and I broke up."

"Why aren't you and that teammate still going at it?"

"You already know. Coach made us kiss and make up. He threatened to cut me from the team if I didn't. He's my best friend now, so it's all moot."

"Ty, are you seeing a pattern here? If you are, tell me how all this relates to the fight you had at the resort."

"It means I'm still angry."

"Yes, but let's just talk about patterns, or cause and effect. Your mom exits your life, you start fighting with your girlfriend. Then you break up with her, and you start in on a teammate… Your turn."

"When someone I'm mad at leaves or puts up boundaries, I take it out on a new person."

"Yes, very good, but would you say you were mad at your mother, or mad about something else during the time you lived with her?"

"Mad at everything."

"That's a great start. We'll leave it there for now. Rome wasn't built in a day."

Ty rolled his eyes. "Just tell me what to think, then. A lot quicker, don't you think?"

"I'm very pleased with your progress, Ty. We have lots of time ahead of us."

Along with another eye roll, Ty let out a loud groan and put his hands on top of his head.

Ty felt like a kid; not only did he have to put up with head-shrinking Ron, he also had to listen to a guidance counsellor grill him on what major he would commit to. Mrs. Jameson was the grandmotherly type, but in appearance only. Ty viewed her as a shark in the water, fixated on its prey. "Ty, you've taken the aptitude tests, we've discussed the results, and you still won't select a major. Can you tell me what might be holding you back?" Ty shrugged. "I guess I just feel maxed out enough keeping up with my classes and the team that I don't have the time to care about it." "Well, I do care, and the school cares. You will have to declare a major by next semester if you want to remain at the U." That comment got Ty's attention. "What?" "Ty, it's all spelled out in the student handbook. So, are you ready to get serious? I can help guide you towards a decision, or at least narrow it down." Ty nodded sheepishly.

"You have an aptitude for things physical and mechanical, and also for math. Your language skills are strong and so are your social skills. That makes you pretty well-rounded, actually. So... maybe that's why you're having trouble deciding!" she laughed, relaxing a bit. After a moment of silence, she began again. "So, here's a list of on-campus volunteer activities and internships. When you come in next week I expect you to have selected one or two. That should tell us something about your interests and where your confidence lies." Ty nodded, took the sheet, and high tailed it out of her office.

Ty was five minutes late to his session with Ron. He practically fell into his chair.
"I'm here!"
Silence.
"Ok, sorry I'm late. I'm here!"
Ron rolled his eyes.
"We'll make up the time at the end of the session. Lucky you, you're my last client of the day."
"Very lucky!" Ty answered sarcastically but with a relaxed half-smile on his face.
"Well, it's time for another card. Do you remember that your parents wrote something on four index cards?"
Ty nodded, then took a card from Ron. As he read the card to himself, he gave a short, quiet laugh. Another slight smile formed on his face.
"Rusty."
Pause.
"I wanted a dog for as long as I can remember. And I'd begged and hassled my parents all the time and they still never got me a dog. My middle school science teacher was trying to find someone to take the class turtle, Rusty, at the end of the year. I wanted it and no one else did, so I took it home on the bus in its glass bowl. The turtle was cool looking with brownish-red designs on its back, and it would stick its head in and out of the shell, but that was about it. My mom kept getting on my case for not taking care of it. She said how I treated Rusty was going to help them decide if I could get a dog or not. I thought that was stupid. It's just a turtle. They're such earthy-crunchy animal lovers, 'animals have feelings, a soul, blah blah blah'. Rusty died at the end of the summer."
"How'd he die? Did you lose him?"

"No. I think he starved to death. I kept hassling them for a dog. I think my mother was about to kill me, literally kill me, then she really flipped out. She actually bought a stuffed dog. It was a miniature collie and she named it Mimi. So, after that, whenever I asked them for a REAL DOG, they would just smile or laugh and say, 'Silly, we *have* a dog.'"

Ty took a pause.

"It gets better. One time I spied my mother sitting on the floor petting the stuffed dog. I made sure she didn't see me and I got the hell out of there."

"What do you think she was thinking or feeling?"

"Probably sad. She and Dad really wanted a dog, too."

"After that, my mother started to treat the dog like a real member of the family. She talked to the dog and brushed her, and didn't try to hide it. One time I sat on the floor with her and 'Mimi' and she said, 'We should get her a dog bed.' I played along and said, 'And bowls for water and food.' She actually got all that stuff and it kept getting weirder. We took her with us on family vacations, she slept on her dog bed on the floor."

"Pretty whacked."

"It was fun, though."

Ron looked Ty in the eyes and smiled.

"BUT WAIT... THERE'S MORE!!!" Ty said in a dramatic tone. They both laughed.

"The story's not over... I finally got a real dog! In high school we had to do community service so I worked at the animal shelter. I moved up the ranks really fast and was training dogs and stuff. Lacy was the best dog, we really clicked. They let me take her home."

"Your parents said 'OK'?"

"Let's just say they didn't say 'no'. My parents flipped over Lacy. We all love her, she's the best. This is the dog that my parents were withholding from me, if you will recall."

"Yeah," Ron nodded.

"Something really cute… Lacy kinda treated the stuffed dog like a real dog. She'd drag her over to her bed and they'd sleep together, and she chewed a lot of stuff, but she was always gentle with Mimi. Pretty freaky, hey?"
Ron patted Ty on the back as he left their session.

Another session with Mrs. Jameson found Ty a bit more comfortable than the previous week. "I looked at the volunteer list. The sports first aid one sounds interesting, since I'm already familiar with what goes on in a team and all." Mrs. Jameson smiled. "Yes, that does sound like a good fit. Your role will be to help the athletes off the field or court, and give them the first line of care, be that an ice pack or a bandage. Then, you will recommend additional treatment as necessary; that could be an ambulance or the campus doctor." "Sounds like a lot of pressure," Ty commented. "You will always have a partner, and lots of training. Plus, you get to watch all the games!" Ty nodded.
So, let's look at the majors list, but you don't have to decide, just give me your reaction to the various majors. She handed him the list. "Art, no way! Literature, no. Teaching, no. Psychology, no with a capital 'N'. Accounting, nope. Pharmacy; that could be cool. Biology, no. Chemistry, too hard… I don't see anything I'm really interested in." "Can you give me some examples, Ty?" "Like, sports management, or advertising or website design." "Ty, at this time we don't offer those programs but you could always transfer." Ty's head shot up. "I'm good here, really. I don't want to leave the team. I'll pick something soon, promise." Mrs. Jameson smiled as she set up their next appointment.

As Thanksgiving approached, Ty decided he'd better let his mother know that he wasn't going to feel obligated to spend the holiday with them. If they were going to run his life, he was going to have to push back... reclaim some of his freedom. Instead of facing an argument with his mother over the phone, he decided to text her.

Hey, Mom, I'm going to hang out with some guys from the team over Thanksgiving break, the ones who live too far to go home. I'm not in the mood to pretend what you're doing is fine with me. I still feel like you're treating me like a little kid. I have cooperated with the therapy, and I am doing a lot better now. I'm not taking my anger out on people anymore, so I should be done with therapy. I'll come home for Christmas if you stop making me go to Ron's. Say hi to Dad. Ty

When Ty walked into Ron's office, he noticed a huge grin on his therapist's face.

"What? Is my fly down?"

Very abruptly, Ron took a deep breath and, smiling, said, "Ok, it's showtime! Lacy is in the building."

Ty's face lit up. He heard a dog barking.

"Carla should be back from their walk, let's go find them. I have to return her to your parents by midnight or she'll turn into a pumpkin."

When Ty finally spotted Lacy, he got down on his knees, and the dog immediately ran into his arms. They wrestled and he kissed the top of her head, and they wrestled some more.

"Oh, my god. This is awesome! Can we take her outside?"

The three went down the stairs out onto the green.

"Where to?" Ron asks.

"Can I show her the field?"

"Ah, yes, the old gridiron. Dogs are famous for their love of football..."

Ty would have none of it. "We're going!"

Ron laughed. "I know."
After a few laps around the field, Ron and Ty stood in place as Ty repeatedly threw a raquetball for Lacy to chase down over and again.

Chapter 17: December

On a gloomy Saturday afternoon, the team warmed up before their home game. There were flurries in the air, but it was warm, and humid. Ty turned in early the night before; he was psyched for this game. They were approaching the end of the season; he had to get serious and make something happen… maybe today.

In the second half of the game, with Ty's team trailing behind, Ty got into formation. They were on defense. The opposing team's quarterback threw a long pass, in Ty's direction. As he went to block, he realized he might have a chance at catching the ball! He raced in, held out his hands in a cradle formation, and the ball landed in his arms. He ran right, then down the field to a touchdown. His head went dizzy, his heart over-racing. Then he heard noise, lots of noise. As he regained his senses, he was being tackled, crushed… kissed? There was a guy kissing him! What the hell? It was Shawn; he had ripped off Ty's helmet and planted a wet one on his lips! Ty laughed, sputtering. "Holy shit, was that an IR?" Shawn punched him in the arm, "You bet, baby!"

Moments later, Ty was hugging his parents. His dad was so excited it looked like he would burst. The special teams coach and the head coach were slapping Ty's back and saying something to his parents. Ty knew this was going to amount to the most important day of his football career. He was under no illusions that he was NFL material, but he was proud, and gratified nonetheless.

Everyone had to get back to work then… the game was not over. For the rest of the game, Ty floated on a cloud, dazed. Lucky for the team, nothing came his way, since he would have missed it anyhow. Life was good.

When Ty was showered and dressed in his street clothes, he decided to find his parents again. Since they had come all this way for his game, it was the least he could do. Plus, his parents didn't hassle him for blowing off Thanksgiving. They called him the night before to wish him a happy holiday and said the door was open if he changed his mind. Ty was relieved they let it go without a fight.

He hugged his mom again and they decided to go out for wings. "Wow, Ty, you must be walking on air!" his dad remarked. "Yeah, talk about being in the right place at the right time!" "Well," his mom interjected, "I'm sure it took focus and skill to take advantage of the situation. You should be very proud." When the food arrived, everyone ate in a contented silence. Before leaving the restaurant, Ty could tell his mother was preparing for another conversation. As predicted, the subject of Christmas came up. "Ty, your dad and I were hoping you'd consider coming home for Christmas… as many or as few days as you like. We'd love to spend the holiday with you." Ty took a deep breath, then exhaled, not ready to answer. His dad filled the silence. "Hey, I could use some help on my brakes… it could be like old times, you know, with your old Subaru?" Ty nodded, unable to suppress a smile as he remembered the good times they had had fixing up his first car. "I'll think about it. Thanks for the invite." His mother nodded, apparently feeling hopeful.

Just before eleven that night, Ty saw his parents off. He made a bee line to the party where everyone on the team had gathered a couple hours earlier. He was greeted and congratulated by several people in succession, all drunk and offering him beer and food. He scanned the room and found Shawn. "Hey, you survived dinner with your folks?" "Yeah, at least we had the game to talk about. I see you're the only semi-sober one here?"

"Don't want to ruin my workout tomorrow," Shawn replied, flexing his biceps. Ty shook his head. They were interrupted by a tap on Ty's shoulder. As he turned around, a female student he vaguely recognized gave him a hug, squealing, "Congrats, Ty! You're the man!"

She was obviously drunk. She grabbed Ty's arm and pulled him off to the side so they could talk privately. "Dance with me, Ty!" Ty hesitated a moment, then answered, "Teresa, you're too drunk to stand up, not to mention dance."

"I'm not drunk," she countered, playfully punching him in the arm. "I was hoping to take you back to my room after." She smiled, trying to look alluring, but instead she just looked dizzy and cross-eyed.

"Some other time, Teresa. Why don't you sit down, and I'll get you a plate and some water." She made a disappointed face, but sat down on the nearest couch to watch the activity. When Ty returned twenty minutes later with pizza and a drink, she was gone.

Ty and Shawn danced and joked with the crowd for a while, then they broke away at the same time and headed towards the door. "You going?" Shawn asked. "Yeah, I'm beat. It's tiring being famous!" Shawn rolled his eyes. "Don't get used to it. Your five minutes of fame will be over in no time. Plus, next week when I break a record they'll forget you exist!" Ty laughed in response as they headed back to the dorm.

"So…" Shawn began, "did I see you get propositioned three, maybe four times tonight, you stud?"

Ty laughed. "Yeah, I guess you have to be really drunk to be into me. One of the girls almost barfed on my sweatshirt!"

"And… you're walking home with me instead of getting lucky. What's that about?"

Ty retorted, "I'm not that desperate! I don't find drunk girls a turn-on. Especially the ones who never gave me the time of day before yesterday's game. Let's just say I prefer my women hard to get."

Shawn guffawed, doubling over. "Ain't that the truth! That's why Ty ain't got no ladies!"

Ty sighed, getting tired of the ribbing. "I wouldn't talk, you're as much a celibate monk loser as I am these days!"

"Who says I didn't get lucky over Thanksgiving break?" Ty's eyebrows shot up.

Shawn and Ty were inseparable during finals week. They studied together, keeping each other honest and focused. "You know, Ty, I've paid for at least four pizzas so far this week, you'd better pony up soon." Ty sighed. "Shut up, I'm trying to study." Ty felt good about being able to help Shawn; he was good at grammar and writing. In lieu of a final exam in his Exposition class, Shawn had a thirty page paper. Ty was his unmerciful critic. "Do you want an A… or do you want a D?" Ty repeated after Shawn complained about Ty's edits for the fourth time. "All I do is rewrite and rewrite, and I only have fifteen pages. Knock it off, Ty, or I'll never finish!" "Ok, I'll back off until you can hand me the thirty pages. Then it's game back on." Shawn rolled his eyes, but he was grateful for Ty's help.

When they took a stretch break an hour later, Shawn asked, "What do you wanna do when finals are over… before I leave for Christmas break? I've got two free days before I head to my mom's." Ty thought for a minute. "Gambling?" Shawn scoffed, "You're broker than broke!" "Strip club?" Ty offered. Shawn rolled his eyes. "I know!" Ty almost shouted. "We can go to Boston, see the BU game on Thursday. Markie lives out there, we can crash at his parents' house." Shawn nodded in approval, then sat back down to his paper. He was glad to have some reward waiting him when all this work was over.

Two weeks later, Ty found himself at his parents' house. He and Shawn and Markie had had a blast in Boston, and he didn't even have to bum any money off the guys. He helped his mother cook, which he actually found himself enjoying. "Ty, this is fun!" his mother said, smiling. "I'm so glad you came home, even if just for a few days. It's great to spend time with you." Ty nodded, but didn't feel comfortable saying anything. He still wasn't sure if he was comfortable there or not. He had let the subject of his forced therapy drop and went home for Christmas without winning that concession. Despite his feelings of resentment, he was having a nice, relaxed time with his mom in the kitchen. They prepared a tofu 'turkey', kale-cranberry-bulgur stuffing loaded with garlic and onions, roasted yams, brussels sprouts, and pumpkin pie. His aunt and two young cousins would join them for the meal.

The next day, Ty and his dad dressed in their oldest clothes to work on the brakes of his father's car. They recalled the fun and mishaps working on the Subaru, laughing often as they worked. Ty played some music he discovered while in college, and his father seemed to like it as well. At times during the repair, there was nothing for Ty to do, so he did most of the talking. He eventually arrived at his agenda for the weekend, to convince his father to do his bidding. "Dad," Ty said in a casual voice, "I've been asking Mom to drop the therapy requirement, 'cause I've been so cooperative, you know, can you help me convince her?" Ty's father grunted as he sat upright to look at his son. "Ty, this is not just your mother's idea. We agreed to it jointly and we still believe it's of great benefit to you." Ty looked at him, disappointed. His father continued. "So, to be clear, I hope that you will continue to work with Ron. This is an opportunity. Your mom and I are seeing a counsellor as well, and I'm getting a lot out of it." Ty looked away, angry. He was glad to be leaving in the morning. He needed some freedom, some space. "Ok, Dad, I get it. You don't trust me yet. I had fun working on the car and all, but don't expect me to come back home for a visit any time soon." Ty's father nodded, not surprised by his son's reaction. "We love you very much, and we want the best for you. I hope that someday you'll come to see that, and we can be closer again."

Chapter 18: January

One cold evening in late January, Ty ran to catch the team bus. As a newly-trained member of the Sports Aid program, he was to shadow a more seasoned member for this evening's women's basketball away-game. He found his mentor, a junior named Ray, chatting it up with the bus driver. Ty considered ditching him and heading toward the party zone of the bus, but decided to do this right. He sat with Ray, who went through a few last minute details. "Don't give ice to everyone who asks for it, YOU decide who needs the ice. We've got some hypochondriacs on this bus! Hypochondriac hotties!" he laughed at his own corny joke. "Don't be surprised if most of their complaints tonight are about broken nails!"

Ty was prepared for a slow night in the first aid department. This job was going to be a piece of cake. He might even get some homework done.

The game was an exciting one. His school was doing great. Their coordinated teamwork, especially in the defense area, was impressive. He noticed a tall, wiry girl with a very pretty face. She played center, and was all business. She didn't let a single shot go in. In the middle of the second half, things took a bad turn for her. As she raised her arms to block an aggressive shot, a player on the opposing team slammed hard into her left shoulder. She did not go down. She stood still, a look of disbelief and shock on her face. Then, the pain set in and as everyone on the court finally noticed what had happened, they cleared a path for Ray and Ty to come to her. Ray said something to the injured player and she followed him over to the cooler and other equipment they had parked in a corner. Ray put a hand gently under her right armpit, helping her to sit down. He called to Ty to get the ice packs and a sling. When Ty returned, he saw Ray look towards the court. "You got this, Ty? Ally's knee must be giving out on her, I'm gonna ask the coach to take her out for a while."

Ty nodded, and approached his patient. She was breathing heavily, and wincing in pain.

"Can we start with some ice? I can strap it to your shoulder."

"Okay," she croaked.

Ty gently applied several ice packs, molding them around her shoulder, neck, and armpit. He kept them in place with ace bandages and then proceeded to apply the sling.

"Ow!!!" she cried.

"Sorry," Ty said. He felt awkward. He hadn't practiced immobilizing a shoulder, only knees and elbows. "I'm new at this. Sorry."

She nodded, closing her eyes. After a moment, she opened them again. "I can't believe this! We just started the damned season!"

"I'm sorry," said Ty. "Maybe the doctor will say it's not as bad as all that. We'll get you to see her in about twenty minutes. Can you hang in there until then?"

"Yeah. The ice is helping. I'm Tasha. Hey, aren't you the guy who did the immaculate reception in the last home game? Pretty amazing, congrats."

Ty nodded, blushing.

The next morning, Ty felt a desperate need to talk to Shawn. He had to wait until their afternoon workout. In between incline and decline bench presses, Ty grilled Shawn for information. "Do you know who she is? Do you know any of her friends? What's she like?" Shawn sighed in annoyance. "Dude, I keep telling you, she's in my Bio class, but I don't know anything about her and I don't know her friends. Why don't you just ask her out and find out for yourself what she's like by hanging out with her?" Ty couldn't admit he was afraid to take the risk. Shawn picked up on the tension. "Ty, get over yourself. I'm pretty sure she'll say yes, if she's not into anyone else. You have nothing to lose." "What about my pride?" "What good is pride if you're still single? Don't be an idiot!" Ty realized he was out of excuses. He was going into battle, fear be damned.

A few days later, Ty shoved a piece of paper into Shawn's hand. "Give that to Tasha for me, since you're in the same class." Shawn grinned. "A love note?" "Just do it. I'll owe you one." Shawn guffawed. "If I kept track of everything you owed me and didn't pay back, I'd be a bitter, bitter man!" Ty rolled his eyes and walked away, confident that his best friend would do him this favor. He was not especially proud of his technique to win Tasha, but he figured all is fair in love and war.

Apparently Shawn had given Tasha Ty's phone number, because he received a text from her several hours later.
My shoulder is feeling better, thanks for asking. But I can see through your Sports Aid act. If you want to ask me out, you'll have to do it in person.
Ty was elated, and very afraid. He returned her message.
You got me. I was just testing out the waters, seeing if you were single. Can you take a walk with me tomorrow at 2? Glad your shoulder is healing. Ty

Ty slept like a log that night, confident that he was the luckiest man alive.

Tasha and Ty munched on sourdough pizza at a little restaurant just off campus. This was the second date Ty managed to entice her to agree to. She seemed very comfortable with him, which helped to grow Ty's confidence. He was falling for her, hard.

"My birthday is next Sunday," Tasha announced.

"Great! Let me take you someplace special. What's your favorite restaurant around here?"

"Actually, Ty, I already have plans."

Ty seemed disappointed. "You have a date?"

She shook her head.

"You're going home for the weekend?"

Tasha spoke. "No, my parents will be in Texas for a conference. I'm treating myself to several luxurious hours at the butterfly exhibit in Portland. Stacie was going to join me, but she cancelled a few days ago." She brightened. "What do you say, will you treat me for my birthday? It'll be fun!"

Ty hesitated, then answered, "Sorry, I'll pass. Sounds like a yawner. No offense, just not my thing."

Tasha smiled wistfully.

"What?" Ty asked.

"You don't have a clue about relationships, do you?"

"What are you talking about? I had a steady girlfriend for three years!"

Tasha shook her head. "One word... Compromise."

"I'm just trying to be honest. I wouldn't be a great sport and I don't want to ruin your fun."

After Tasha swallowed her bite of pizza, she replied. "Well, Ty, if you want to get to know me, spend time with me, you may want to re-think that. One of the reasons I broke up with Lawrence was he never wanted to do anything that interested me, even though I made an effort to do things he liked."

"Let me guess," Ty broke in, "he taught you to shoot pool."

"Exactly. It didn't interest me in the least, but I gave it a go, for him."

Ty laughed. "And now, you're a pool shark, or so I hear!" Tasha moved closer to him, whispering in his ear, "I'll let you beat me at one round if you take me to see the butterflies."

"Deal." Ty was smiling.

As they got up to leave, Ty took Tasha's hand. They both felt amazing.

Ty was still dreading the butterfly exhibit, so he made sure his phone was fully charged and he packed his homework and some body building magazines to keep him occupied. He felt embarrassed that he didn't own a car. It would take some getting used to, riding shotgun in Tasha's car, but she was worth it.

Once they pulled up to the large glass building, Tasha gasped. "Oh, it's gorgeous! A tropical jungle, and it looks really big!" After Ty paid for their tickets, they navigated a set of double doors, feeling a powerful fan at their backs, used to keep the winged creatures from escaping the habitat area. The warm, moist air was a welcome change from the winter cold.

Ty could not hide his relief and enthusiasm, once inside. He blurted out, "Cool. They're alive!"

Tasha just stared at him for a moment. "What were you expecting?"

"I thought it was going to be a bunch of glass cases displaying dead butterflies with their wings pinned open."

They both laughed. Tasha knew then that it was going to be a great day.

Ty put his backpack on a bench and never opened it after that. Tasha unpacked some sophisticated-looking camera equipment as Ty fiddled with the camera settings on his cell phone. Tasha stood up. "My lenses are all fogged. It'll be a while before they come up to temp. Let's just wander around. Oh, Ty! Look at that one!" She pointed out a large black beauty with large white spots. Butterflies were flying around everywhere. Many were up towards the glass ceiling, others among the plants, flowers, and trees, and others, still, walked around in the puddles on the ground. They had to watch every step.

"Oh, my God, Ty! Did you see that green one?"

"Yeah, and the shiny blue ones are cool," Ty added.

"What's this?" Tasha asked to no one in particular, examining a butterfly perched on a branch. "Most of its wings are transparent, like they're made of glass. Just the edges look painted!"

Ty watched Tasha in her excitement. Her face was relaxed and joyful at the same time. She was like a kid at Christmas. She was beautiful. Ty couldn't keep his eyes off her.

She broke away from him then, heading back to her equipment, which she assembled quickly after selecting a lens. "This is a macro lens. I can capture all the fine detail on the wings with this. Like with this large black butterfly, it'll probably look like fish scales, I can get so close up."

Ty decided to give the artist some room to work. He wandered off on his own. He noticed papayas ripening on a tall tree, and a green gecko hugging a tree trunk. He couldn't stop himself, he started to think about his mom, how she would love this place. He decided to take some photos and send them to her. He really got into it and didn't notice the time flying by.

Tasha approached him to show off a few of her most recent shots.

"Wow!" exclaimed Ty. "You really know what you're doing."

"Thanks. My dad taught me everything I know about photography."

"Everything?" Ty raised an eyebrow.

"Well, not to brag, but I think I'm a little more creative in setting up my shots."

"Like that one," Ty interrupted, pointing at the display screen on her camera. "You just show part of its body, not the whole thing."

"Exactly! You know how to flatter me," she teased, stealing a kiss on his cheek.

Ty looked into her eyes. "Tasha, I'm really glad I came. I'm sorry for being a total jerk about it before."

"All is forgiven... if you give me a kiss!"

Ty readily agreed. This was definitely the best day he'd had in a very long time. As they broke off the embrace, Tasha gasped. "Ty! One landed on your shoulder!" Ty craned his neck to see it and was a little startled to see the large iridescent blue marvel sitting on his shirt.

"Don't move!" Tasha cried, as she set up the shot. "I'm gonna do just the butterfly first, then man with beast!" she laughed. Approximately fifteen clicks of the camera later, Tasha called out to Ty, "Relax, don't look so nervous. Look at the butterfly...yes, that's better, oh, that's gonna be great!" She got a beautiful shot, capturing Ty's face full of wonder.

"If you post that on Facebook, we're OVER!" Ty called to her in mock anger. They both laughed, and Ty's friend flew away.

After four hours in the conservatory, they noticed their hunger and headed over to the eating area. They looked at each other's photos as they ate hot dogs.

"Which one's your favorite?" Ty asked.

"All of them!" Tasha laughed. "I love the green and black one, and the yellow striped one, but, I have to say, the pale orange little guy here," she said, pointing to the screen, "is the star. His color deepens against the green leaves, gorgeous!" Tasha was beaming. "Let's go back in for a while before calling it a day, okay?"

"Hey, no problem. Take as long as you want." Ty answered, without hesitation.

"That's the spirit!" Tasha said, as she kissed his cheek again. "Ugh! You got mustard on my face!"

Tasha laughed, with a devilish look in her eyes. "Do you want me to kiss it off, or not?"

Ty kept the game going, pretending to be immune to Tasha's tempting offer. "No, thanks. I'll just go to the men's room for some soap."

Tasha pulled on his sleeve. "Don't you dare!" she laughed.

It was all they could do to keep the next kiss G-rated.

Chapter 19: February

Ty felt out of sorts since the football season ended. He figured his ego was wrapped up in being on the team. He still worked out with Shawn on a regular basis, so that helped somewhat. He resolved to join an intramural basketball team the following week. Although it was past the deadline, he hoped they would at least include him as a sub.
Since Ty felt too distracted to do his homework, he composed an e mail to his parents.

Dear Mom and Dad,
The official season is over but I'm still wicked busy. I'm in the Sports Aid program. I've learned some first aid for any injuries that happen during practice or games, and I'm an 'observer' the rehab gym twice a week making sure the jocks do their rehab. Like a babysitter, ha ha. My advisor set this up since I'm leaning toward either Sports Med or Pharmacy as a major. They're going to decide in the fall if there's enough kids to start up the Sports Med major. I hope so.
So far, as a Sports Aid volunteer, I've wrapped knees and ankles and cleaned up skinned knees and elbows, that kind of stuff. In the gym, I really like working with Mac. He's a vet here on the G.I. Bill. He's not on a university team (yet), but they let him use the rehab room. His arms are ENORMOUS. He plays wheelchair rugby on the weekends on a team out of Portland. I go watch whenever I can. He's really cool.
This job doesn't pay, of course, but it does have its perks. I met someone, her name is Tasha and we've been hanging out for about a month. She torqued her shoulder and so we're going to do some winter hiking as part of her attempt to keep in good cardio shape for basketball. She's probably out for the rest of the season, but her coach is sure she'll be in again next year.
See you on the 17th.
Love, Ty

During his session with Ron that month, Ty could not suppress his goofy grin.

Toward the end of the session, Ron decided to have some fun. "Oh my dear blessed soul, Ty, are you in love?"

Ty stomped his foot. "Why can't a man have his private life? You know what, it's none of your damned business!"

Ron laughed. "I see... the relationship is too new... too fragile, like fine crystal, a baby bird, a soufflé hot out of the oven..."

"Hate to interrupt you, Ron, but time's almost up, thank God."

"Ok, I guess I'll just have to fill in the blanks myself... until you cave!"

They both laughed as Ty got up to leave, happy to be away from the pressure to reveal his inner secrets.

Chapter 20: March

Ty had convinced Shawn and a few other teammates to join recreational basketball. It turned out they were in desperate need of more players and were on the verge of disbanding. They now had enough players to scrimmage, and they met twice a week. Between classes, this new team, his Sports Aid gig, and dating Tasha, his days and nights were full and he felt happier than he had in a very long time.

One Thursday night on the basketball court, Ty's patience was tested. Each time he went up court for a shot, the guy assigned to his defense continually crossed the line. Elbows in the ribs, shoulder checks, but with such force it reeked of poor sportsmanship. At one point Ty was ready to let the guy have it, but he reminded himself that if he made the situation worse they might kick him off the team. He broke away from this player named Mike, squatted down and took several deep breaths to calm himself. It was a typical stance for athletes, so it did not raise suspicion that anything was bothering him.

The next time the group met, Ty had hoped that guy Mike would be absent, but he was there, all revved up. He approached Ty. "Hey, I'm Mike." He extended his hand to Ty. Ty looked at him but did not shake his hand. "Ok, I was a jerk last week. I was having a wicked bad day and sports helps me get the junk out, you know what I mean?" Ty walked away, unwilling to be this kid's therapist. During the game, everyone had a great time and Mike was a more respectful player and did not bother Ty at all. He was still assigned to cover Ty, but he acted like a different person. When Ty was ready to head back to the dorm, Mike said, "Hey, I hope we're ok. I won't act like a jerk anymore on the court… but I can't guarantee off court…" He laughed. Ty looked Mike in the eye. "Yeah, we're ok. Name is Ty." They finally did shake hands, and as Ty walked away, he was glad he had let Mike's offenses go. He realized it's better to have friends than enemies. This was similar to the problems he had had with the kid at his summer job, and they had become friends after they'd gotten over themselves.

Ty flopped down in front of Ron. "Trouble in paradise… already?" Ron inquired.
"Yeah, it's not monumental, but you can help me work something out."
Ron nodded, patiently waiting for Ty to fill in the details.
"It seems like we're dancing around each other… trying to act cool, but all I want to do is just spend more time with her. Instead, we only see each other a couple times a week, and it feels like this contest to see who has more of a life."
"Do I follow right that you and your sweetheart are filling up your time with independent activities?"
"Yeah, it's like we're trying to prove we don't really need each other, that we're not going to be one of those lame couples that tracks each other's moves."

"Ah, the fear of crash and burn. I know it well. You want to spend every waking moment with your new found love, but you don't want it to implode."

"You got it, old man. I guess you've been there, done that?"

"That's right. It's a perfectly normal concern. But, you know what, you miss out on a lot of times together. Tell me… what do you want?"

"What do you mean?"

"Literally, how do you want things to go with this young lady… what's her name?"

"Tasha. I want to see her more, but I don't want either of us to feel like we can't do stuff with our own friends."

"Compromise. Is she a good communicator? Maybe you can talk this out."

"Yeah, all girls are good communicators. And she's real fair and mature. It just would feel like an unnatural, uncomfortable conversation."

"Well, if you're happy with the status quo…"

Ty exhaled loudly. "Of course I'm not. So, tell me what to say."

Ron laughed. "You're not getting off that easy. Plus, you're not the one paying me. You can do this work yourself. I have another…. twenty minutes, plenty of time!"

Ty rolled his eyes, but realized he needed Ron's help. He was willing to do what it takes to keep this new girl interested. "Okay, I want to be clear with her, but I don't want to sound lame."

Ron waited.

Ty began, "Hey, Tasha, I know we both have our own friends and we want to keep hanging out with them, but I was wondering if you'd be interested in us hanging out together a little more often, maybe three or four times a week instead of one or two?"

Ron beamed. "You're on to something, Junior! That was very clear, very unthreatening, and not lame in the least!"

"You mean it didn't sound needy?"

"No, because you made it clear you still want to have time with your friends."

Ty's shoulders relaxed. "Ok, I think I'm good. I'll talk to her when I see her Friday night."

"Go get 'em, Tiger!" Ron cheered, as Ty shook his head in mock embarrassment.

Chapter 21: April

Ty went Sunday evening to Tasha's apartment to watch a movie. They were still getting to know each other, and he often hesitated over revealing personal information. They had only gotten together once since the butterfly outing, a quick supper two weeks ago. Both of them had been busy with their teams and midterm exams and papers. When she turned off the television, Tasha hugged a pillow and turned towards Ty. "Did you like the movie?" "Pretty creepy." Ty admitted. "Yeah, but love triumphed in the end… that was beautiful!" Ty rolled his eyes and patted Tasha's knee. "Hey, don't make fun of me, Ty… I can't help it if I love my romance!" "Well, I hope you'll let me sweep you off your feet," Ty replied, with mischief in his eyes. "We'll see… you have your work cut out for you, since I have high standards!" Ty held Tasha's hand and they sat in relaxed silence for a few moments.
Tasha took the lead. "Tell me about your family, do you have brothers and sisters, that sort of stuff." "It's just me… and my parents," Ty offered. Tasha would have to draw details out of him, so she continued, "So, what was it like growing up, any fond memories, vacations, pets…?" "I hung out with my dad sometimes, and we have a great dog named Lacy." "Cool," Tasha answered. She waited for Ty to go on. "I don't really know what else to tell you… how about you?" "Ok, well, my parents are great, and I have a sister and two baby brothers. We live in New Hampshire, as you know, and my mom is an attorney for the restaurant industry, mainly. My dad is a software engineer, but he's been laid off for a couple of years now… I think he's retired. No one wants to hire a guy with gray hair!" Ty nodded in sympathy.

After a pause, Ty picked up the ball. "So, should we plan our first hike?" He was hoping Tasha would say yes; she hadn't brought it up in a long time and he was worried she was losing interest in spending time with him. They hadn't even talked about dating exclusively yet... He wasn't getting any signals that she was ready. Maybe a hike in the fresh air would seal the deal. "Yeah," Tasha answered, "I am so ready! Let's go as soon as we get a fifty degree day." "Hopefully that's really soon, because I want to kiss you on the mountain top!" Ty said, then leaned over for a kiss. Tasha was interested. Ty was happy and relieved.

Chapter 22: May

On a Saturday morning in early May, Tasha picked up Ty, two cups of steaming coffee in the cup holders of her car. Ty was waiting outside, ready, but rubbing his bleary eyes. After he climbed in, he commented, "You really were serious... seven o'clock!? Did you go to bed at 8pm or something?"

"And, good morning to you, too!" Tasha grinned a perky wide-awake grin to annoy him further.

He rolled his eyes, then turned to face her for a hug and a kiss. "Will you be offended if I sleep on the drive?"

"Not at all," she replied, "as long as you let me listen to my music in peace."

"Chill-out?" Ty asked.

"Hindi fusion today, relaxing, but energizing at the same time."

"Ok," Ty replied, "I'll block it out if it gets too wild, I'm still really bushed."

"Nighty-night," she cooed, and they were on their way.

Forty-five minutes later, they arrived at their destination. The hiking trail started at a picnic area, and they selected the four-mile route marked 'moderate difficulty'. They walked on soft pine needles for a long stretch, holding hands and taking a leisurely pace to start out.

They then approached a rock face on their left, and Ty let out a 'whoop' and proceeded to climb it. There were just enough natural footholds in the rock that he had no trouble reaching the top in under two minutes. He ran down its mossy top back to where Tasha was waiting. He beat his chest gorilla-style as Tasha rolled her eyes.

"You just wait until my shoulder is healed, I'll put your climbing to SHAME!"

Ty laughed, and grabbed her in a bear hug. "I can't wait, babe, bring it on!"

They both laughed and then started back on the trail.

"We should go to Acadia this summer." she said, dreamily.
It's gorgeous. Tons of great hiking, on pink granite with
ocean views at the top."
"Sounds like a plan," Ty answered, enthusiastically.
"Just promise me one thing, King Kong…"
Ty was all ears.
"That you'll be brave enough to try the LOBSTAH ice cream!"
He doubled over, laughing. "Like that's gonna happen…
gross!"
Tasha was quiet for a moment, and Ty realized she was
feeling superior again. "God, Tash, you're serious!?! How am
I gonna keep up with you?"
She smiled. "Lobster ice cream is just the beginning, if you
want to hang with me!"
Ty took her hand and they picked up their pace.
After a few moments, Ty jerked his head toward her, alarmed
to hear her gasp, "Oh, Ty, Lady's Slippers! I LOVE the pink
ones!" They stopped to squat down at a mossy, wet area full
of pink and white flowers, a type of orchid that looks like a
balloon with a few long leaves draped over the top. "When I
was a kid," Tasha explained, "we'd go into the woods with
our Science teachers every spring and they'd tell us we would
go to jail if we picked that special flower. It was protected."
Ty pulled out his phone and took several shots.
Tasha smiled at his thoughtfulness. When he was done, she
pulled him to her for a long kiss. When they came up for air,
Ty beat his chest again in triumph.
"You're almost as crazy as me," she said, "You might just be a
keeper."
Ty smiled and grasped her hand as they resumed their hike.
He was feeling great. Excited, happy, loved, hopeful. These
were the times he remembered treating Regina so badly when
they started college. He thought about writing her an
apology.

The two climbed over what seemed like a giant's pile of rocks spilled on the ground. Tasha in the lead, she let out a scream. "Don't move!" she said, as she gingerly descended the last of the boulders onto solid ground. She squatted down and told Ty to watch his step. A tiny neon orange salamander was resting on some moss.

A short distance later, on a bed of pine needles, they made their final ascent, reaching the summit. The views were stunning. A valley filled with pines in the foreground linked to a farm field beyond. A river or stream ran along one side of the field, with civilization on the other side, with tiny swimming pools and Monopoly-sized houses. They kept their gaze mainly on the peaceful stand of trees.

"Did you bring the snacks?" Tasha asked, rubbing her hands together expectantly. "Tell me you brought something yummy, I'm starved!"

Ty was proud of himself. He had done his homework with the eagerness of a person newly in love. He pulled the booty out of his pack as they sat on a large rock together. Grapes, carrots and dip, cranberry-walnut and blueberry muffins emerged from his bag. Tasha pulled the napkins and water bottles out from the side pockets.

"Yeah, you did good, Private," Tasha joked, as she reached for a blueberry muffin. "Thanks, Ty, it's perfect."

After they ate, Ty cleared his throat. "I've been looking forward to this time with you ever since you brought up the idea. It's cool to get away from it all… to have you all to myself."

Tasha leaned her head on his shoulder. She laughed, "Now, if you tell me you made the muffins yourself, I might just fall in love!"

Ty was surprised by her comment. It sounded promising. He looked at her. "I can learn how to make muffins… if you know what I mean."

"Why don't you do that, cowboy, it just might move our relationship along."

He slipped his arm around her and they gazed contentedly down at the view below. Then, out of the blue, he picked her up and spun her around.

"I don't give a crap about muffins, I'm just gonna say it and I don't care if you're ready or not, Tasha, I LOVE you."

He spun her around again. They both laughed and she gave him a kiss. "Give me a little time, Ty, but I like what you're saying." She looked at him warmly. She wasn't the least bit uncomfortable. She gestured for Ty to lay down on the grass. She reached over and grabbed some grapes and fed them to him.

"Mmmm..." he murmured, closing his eyes. She ran her hands over his face, his hair, and kissed him again. The devilish look returned to her face, "Last one down the mountain is a rotten egg!"

Ty couldn't resist. He packed up quickly and ran to catch up. On the ride home, they didn't talk much, mostly listened to the music. Ty took out a notebook, deciding to write the letter to Regina. He was a few minutes into the project when Tasha commented, "You sure look intense over there. What are you doing?"

"I'm starting a letter of apology."

Tasha didn't press for details, but Ty decided to give more. "I treated my last girlfriend pretty crappy near the end, and I want to tell her I'm sorry and that I've changed."

"You want to win her back?" Tasha asked.

Ty couldn't tell if she was serious or not, but he decided to take her comment at face value and answer her reassuringly. "No, Tash. I want to be with you. It's just that being with you makes me think about it and I want to tell her I realize now that I took her for granted, that I'm sorry I hurt her."

Tasha smiled. "Ty, I think that's awesome. I'm really having an influence on you!" She grinned like a cheshire cat.

"I guess so," Ty answered, and playfully slapped the side of her leg. "We have to grow up sometime, right?"

"You bet," Tasha replied, then returned her focus on the road, still smiling.

Chapter 23: June

"Hey, Ron. Coach says I've got a real good chance of winning the Athlete Scholar Award this year."
"Excellent. I've heard of it. It's a real big deal. Banquet, speech, the works. They pay all your tuition and expenses for junior and senior year?"
"Hey, would you be willing to be my character reference? They ask for a short letter of recommendation. I need to get them from my coach and favorite professor, too."
"Of course, Ty. I can certainly say good things about your character… maybe not so much a year ago, but now, absolutely."
Ty gave a sheepish grin.
"Awesome. Thanks! I'll e mail you the form."

June seemed like a month of unending rain, so the first dry Saturday that came around, Tasha asked Ty to start running with her. "How about a little trail running, my dear?" Ty suggested. "There are some trails behind the park, not too hilly, maybe two miles one way?" Tasha thought for a minute. "You don't think I'll twist an ankle? I'm a city girl, you know." Ty reassured her, "I'll blaze the trail, that way I'll twist my ankle instead of you, and then you can carry me back to the health center." She rolled her eyes, then made up her mind. "I'm in; sounds fun."

The soft forest floor felt good on Tasha's legs; much easier on her knees than pavement or the track. It was peaceful and quiet, and reminded her of her hikes with Ty. Ty's legs were longer than Tasha's, and several times he ran ahead, out of sight. When she finally caught up with Ty, he was drinking from his water bottle. "I can't keep up with you, Ty." Ty wasn't sure if Tasha was upset or just stating the facts. "Tash, do you mind that I'm going at my own pace? If you wanted to talk while we run, I could slow down so we could run together." "Thanks for asking, Ty. Actually, it's probably best to each go at our own pace. Let's walk together a couple miles during our cool down." "That sounds great. Whoever wants to quit first just flag the other down." Ty was glad she wasn't upset that he went ahead during this run. He kicked himself for not asking her beforehand.

When Ty was spent, he found Tasha and they walked together, mostly talking about how hungry they were. "I could eat a moose!" Ty bellowed. "I didn't eat much for breakfast, didn't want to get a side cramp." Tasha agreed, "I could eat five moose! Plus an ice cream sundae for dessert!" Ty was glad Tasha was filled with gusto. She wasn't delicate or picky or constantly dieting. She felt so real to him, so true to herself.

"How about I make you buckwheat banana pancakes, and if you're good, we can put ice cream on top?" Ty offered. "You just won about five million brownie points, my friend!" Tasha smiled.

At the end of July, Ty came into Ron's office, chest puffed up and beaming with pride.

"I won!"

"Come again?" Ron asked.

"The scholar athlete award!"

Ron rose to shake Ty's hand. "Congratulations, that's wonderful, Ty!"

"So, can you come to the awards dinner, Ron? I'd really appreciate it if you'd come, be my guest of honor."

"I might be talked into it… What are they serving?"

Ty rolled his eyes and Ron laughed, rubbing his stomach. "I like my free meals to be GOOD!"

They both laughed.

Ty's expression grew serious as they sat down. "You know what this means, Ron?" He didn't wait for an answer. "It means I'm a free man. I don't have to keep coming here, no offense, and I don't have to play by my parents' stupid rules. I've got a free ride the rest of my college career. I don't need their stupid money!"

Ty got up and started pacing.

"Ty, I realize this is an exciting event in your life, but how about you take some time to process it before flying off the handle?"

"Flying off the handle?!? Do you think this has been a picnic for me? My parents are on some crazy power trip, treating me like a puppet, I have to do what they say, well, that's over!"

"All I ask is you just give it a few days before you do anything rash."

"Rash? You mean, tell my parents exactly how I feel? That I resent all they've put me through since the day I arrived at this school? No, I'm not being rash, I've had these thoughts for a long time; now I have the cash to back it up! I'm a free man!"

They sat in silence for a moment.

"Ron, there must have been a time in YOUR life when you didn't appreciate your parents running the show."

"You're right, Ty, money is power, but I truly believe your parents are not on a power trip. They want what's best for you and for you to take advantage of this opportunity for counseling."

"Well, Ron, I'm just not in the mood anymore. Again, no offense, but I'm out of here."

Ron took a deep breath. "You're right, this is not a prison. But, I hope you will make the right decision and come back next month."

"I'm sorry, Ron. I'm doing this for me. I still would really like to see you at the banquet."

"Send me the information and I'll sleep on it."

Ty nodded and turned to leave, only twenty minutes into their session.

Back at his dorm, Ty composed an e mail to his parents.

Dear Mom and Dad,
Life can be very ironic. You thought you could control me, but I am now a free man. I don't need your money or your stipulations. I've just won a free ride for the rest of my college career, so you can take your little experiment and shove it. I don't appreciate you treating me like a lab rat. What kind of parents do that? I think maybe you two are the ones who need serious counseling. If you want to have any contact with me, I need an apology first.
Ty

Ty texted Shawn and then headed over to his room. Shawn wasn't ready for him yet. "Hey, man, I'm gonna shower, then you can ask me whatever you're gonna ask me." Ty paced as his best friend took a decade in the steamy shower. He couldn't wait, so he started yelling through the door. "So, let's get wasted tonight!" No answer. "I'm talking about celebrating my freedom!" A few minutes later, Shawn opened the bathroom door, wearing just his boxers. He filed past Ty to his bureau to get more clothes.

"Ty, you sound like a little kid. What are you talking about, 'freedom from mommy and daddy'?"

Ty sighed, "They've been putting me through hell, and now I'm free; it's not rocket science." Shawn turned around to face Ty, looking him square in the eye. "You know, I'd kill for my parents to still be in love, hell, to actually be on speaking terms, and for them to take an interest in my life. You don't know when you have it good. In fact, I think your life is pretty great right about now. You have parents that love you, you're getting a college education, you have a hot and classy girlfriend, you're healthy…" Ty turned his back in a huff, feeling tempted to punch the wall. Shawn finished his piece, "You're on your own tonight, kid." Ty could feel his anger rising even more. "Suit yourself, grandma!" Ty yelled in reply, and stormed out of the dorm.

Ty was nervous as he entered the banquet hall. All the award winners were required to say a few words upon receiving their plaques. He had practiced his lines with Shawn, after having apologized for his attitude the other day. Shawn didn't suggest any changes to the wording. He focused on Ty's facial expressions, telling him to look more friendly and relaxed. Ty wasn't feeling anything of the sort lately. But, he decided, he could fake it. This award and the new freedom it brought him were worth it.

He sat with Shawn, Tasha, his coaches, and Ron at a table close to the podium. His parents approached Ty, gave congratulatory hugs, but didn't speak because they knew Ty was not thrilled to see them there. Ty surprised them when he said, "I'm glad you came, even though I didn't invite you, it's cool." His parents smiled and went back to their table. They enjoyed their meals and all chattered away for almost an hour. As the wait staff cleared the plates, Ty got nervous all over again. His palms were sweaty and his stomach cramped. The college athletic director got up to introduce the program. "Welcome, coaches, athletes, friends, and, especially, family. We are so proud to honor our finest scholar athletes this year. Please welcome me in a warm round of applause for all our candidates and winners."

When the room quieted down, he continued, directing each student in turn to shake his hand, accept their award, and speak at the podium. Ty was third in line. When his turn came, he was as ready as he would ever be. He focused his eyes on Shawn, assuming he would be the safest, least threatening person to train his gaze on. He was supposed to look out on the audience, Shawn had coached. Ty cleared his throat.

"I want to thank my coaches for their awesome training. And, for their faith in me. They gave me a second chance and I didn't let them down. I'm proud of my record. But I've learned something much more important, that I value more than my personal moment of glory. It has little to do with football, but everything to do with sports, this school, and, believe it or not, humility and service. By participating in the Sports Aids program, I've learned the value of teamwork. Everyone on the team, from the star player to the coaches to the equipment manager, everyone is essential to both the success of the team and the building of a family. I feel more connected to this school, the staff, and the students, because of my service in Sports Aids. Instead of hoping all eyes were on me, I found myself caring about the safety of the athletes, and cheering them on in good times and bad. I felt proud to be a part of something bigger than myself. Thank you."

JUNIOR YEAR

Ty did not show up for his scheduled therapy appointment with Ron.

Ty headed over to Tasha's apartment after he finished writing draft after draft of an application letter for his internship. He was ready to relax, veg out, and snuggle with his honey. He brought a pizza and was greeted appreciatively by Tasha. "Come in, pizza boy. My boyfriend will be busy for hours, so you and I can fool around if you want." Ty joined in on the act. "Is he that football stud, Ty Something?" "Why, yes he is… but he won't have a clue if we have a little fun." Ty retorted, "I don't know. You're awful hot and I sure am tempted, but I don't want to get pounded into the ground by that football god." Tasha bent over, laughing. She made a vomiting gesture to indicate her opinion of Ty's performance. "I guess I'm not worth the risk. In that case, you'd best leave right now." Ty responded in mock horror. "Ok, ok, you're totally worth getting murdered. You're worth everything to me, in fact." He pulled her close. He was done playing the delivery boy game.

As they ate their pizza, Tasha said, "Ty, have you given any more thought about reconciling with your parents?" Ty closed his eyes in frustration. "Tash, I just want to relax! Can we please skip this conversation?" She responded calmly, half expecting the reaction she had gotten. "Sure, Ty. I'm here if you want to talk it out." "I already did with Shawn. He's been lecturing me and guilting me. He hasn't worn me down yet, but he's sure working on it, so please, don't gang up on me, too." "I'm sorry, I didn't mean to make you feel that way." Ty looked in her eyes. "No, you weren't being pushy. I was just letting off steam. I'm sorry." He leaned over for a kiss. "Yum, pepperoni!" Ty laughed.

Tasha and Ty pooled their money and cleared their schedules and headed out for a mini vacation at Acadia National Park. They rented a tiny cottage with no private bathroom, but it was perfect for a couple in love. "We can rough it for two nights," Tasha said, optimistically. It was drizzling when they arrived in Bar Harbor. "I guess a hike is off for now," Tasha said, disappointed. "I hope it dries up soon!" "We can start sampling the food and that nasty lobster ice cream you've been talking about non stop!" They both laughed. After dumping their bags in the tiny cabin, they headed out on foot. They found a restaurant with outdoor seating and a roof overhead. Ty ordered clam chowder and blueberry pie; Tasha started to order, but was distracted by something licking her leg. She gasped, then looked under the table to find a tiny dog sniffing and licking her skin. "So cute!" she said, crisis over. That's when they started noticing other dogs. Some were tied up outside the eating area, and two large dogs were lying on the floor next to their owners' tables. The wait staff brought around water bowls and dog biscuits. "Wow," Ty said, next time we'll take Lacy!"

They enjoyed their lunch, and as they left, Ty took a photo of a sweet black Lab who was laying on her belly, legs stretched out behind her, and front paws crossed. The owners took notice and the woman said, "That will be fifty cents, please, and a dollar if you want an autograph!" They all laughed and agreed that Acadia was a great place to have fun and relax.

They killed the afternoon at Thunder Hole, a rocky area of the shore where the waves rushed into a tight area between two pink granite boulders, creating high spray and a thunderous sound. The tide was right and the couple was glad to witness this attraction at its prime. There were hand rails on the stairs leading down to the water, and between the drizzle and the ocean spray, they were glad the rails were there. Tasha was talking a mile a minute and didn't notice until too late, when she got drenched by the spray. She screamed, then laughed as she hugged Ty, in mock fear. "My hero!" she joked, but Ty enjoyed the chance to hold her close and wouldn't let her go. He finally loosened his grip and they looked back out onto the dark blue ocean, his arm around her shoulder.

They walked for a while along the side of the road that hugged the coastline, feeling all their cares melt away. Tasha remembered something. "It's time for your treat!" Ty knew exactly what she meant and groaned. "I'll go take a look, but I make NO PROMISES!" Tasha wouldn't take no for an answer. She took his hand and dragged him up with street to the ice cream shop. As they entered, the smell of sugar from the ice cream, the waffle cones, and the salt water taffy was overpowering. They got in a very long line and craned their necks, trying to read the labels on the gallon containers in the glass cases. "I'm gonna try blueberry cheesecake!" Tasha exclaimed. Ty turned to her, "After you have your share of the lobstah!" Tasha smiled devilishly. "I've already paid my dues. You're the newbie, not me!" Ty laughed. "Since when do you make the rules?" Tasha ignored that comment, convinced she was going to change her boyfriend's life for the better with this new experience. When it was their turn to order, Tasha ordered for both of them. "I'll have two scoops of blueberry cheesecake in a bowl, and he'll have one scoop of lobster and one scoop of… Ty, what else do you want?" "Anything that will wipe out the lobster flavor… how about triple chocolate?" They both laughed and took their ice cream outside, away from the crowds. They found a bench near a few trees. The drizzle had ended. Ty stared at his two dishes of ice cream. "One bite, that's all I promised." Tasha nodded encouragingly. Ty took a small amount on his spoon, making sure to grab some of the lobster meat. As he stuck his tongue out to meet the scary dessert, he tasted a sweat cream vanilla. "Not bad, so far," he said. Then, he put the spoon in his mouth and started chewing. The lobster was rubbery, but inoffensive, and even a little sweet. "Hey, not bad!" Tasha began to exhale and smile. "I told you so!" Ty ignored her comment, not willing to concede. He did, however, take a few more bites before he found refuge in the chocolate. "Welcome to the club," Tasha said, giving him a pat on the back.

Ty woke earlier than Tasha the next morning, and checked the weather on his phone. Five percent precipitation. He was eager to tell Tasha the good news. Over a breakfast of omelets and popovers with blueberry jam, the couple planned their day. "If we want to do Cadillac Mountain, we should leave soon because it's a long ways up," Tasha offered. Ty had no frame of reference, so he let Tasha plan out their hikes for the day. They found a parking spot near the trailhead and started up. They passed through mossy pine forest areas, and climbed pink granite boulders that felt like a desolate lunar landscape. After two hours of steady climbing and one water break, they reached the summit. It was a large expanse and several people were walking around, exploring and enjoying the views. The Cranberry Islands were visible as the sky was clear and a beautiful blue. The pair huddled together and stood for a long while, appreciating the beauty. The fresh air, the openness of the area, made Ty feel free. "Thank you," he said. "This is awesome." Tasha nodded, pleased that the couple was finding things in common to enjoy and appreciate.

On the very last day of August, Ty had a change of heart and begged Ron's receptionist to squeeze him in. She found him an open slot.
Ron was very relieved to see Ty, but tried his best to conceal it.
"Why did you come back to therapy, Richie Rich? They don't have much to hold over you any more."
"Because I know they have their reasons for this deal, even though I can't comprehend them."
"But you're a FREE MAN!!! Why do you care?"
Pause.
"I just do."
Ron exhaled audibly. "Good man."
Ron took a moment to breathe, suppressing a sob of relief and joy. He tried to hide it with a cough.

"So, tell me all about your new plans, are you moving out of the dorm into some swinging crib?"

Ty rolled his eyes. "At least choose slang from the same CENTURY in the same sentence!"

Ron held up his hand, guilty as charged. "That's part of my charm!"

Ty exhaled with resignation. "I met you too late, there's no hope for you."

They laughed.

"I think I'll stay in the dorm one more year, then find some roommates for senior year. It's not like I'm rolling in dough. Just enough to get by. If I get a sponsor or something, then things would happen, but I doubt that's going to come my way."

"What do you say I buy you a burger?"

"A man's gotta eat," Ty shrugged.

"Especially a free man!"

On the phone with his mother, Ty decided to face the elephant in the room. "Mom, I'm still seeing Ron. Even though you can't control me any more, I decided to play your game."

After a long silence, his mother replied, "Thank you, Ty, we love you so much."

"I thought you'd back down once you heard about the scholarship, but that thought didn't last long. You're bull headed, just like me."

His mother laughed. "Maybe we can stop butting heads and just enjoy each other."

"Good night, Mom. I'll see you next week." Ty replied and hung up.

"Richie Rich is back for more masochistic torture."
Ron gave a slight smile.
"You can pick a card this month if you like."
"Yeah, here we go again," moaned Ty in mock agony.
Ron fanned out the cards.
"Just give me one already."
"Rude. You're paying for my burger tonight."
Ty read the card aloud, "Heimlich."
"Who made this card, my Dad?"
Ron nodded, pointing to his nose.
Ty laughed a little, to himself. He took another deep breath.
"Come on, I'm dying of curiosity."
"Leave it to Dad to pick the defining moment of our family."
Ron gave Ty a quizzical look, inviting him to continue.
"We were at the beach. All three of us, eating a picnic dinner
Mom had packed for us. It was sunset, we always went to the
beach after four pm because it was free parking. Guess who
was the cheapskate... Mom, and I think I've inherited it from
her, unfortunately!"
They both laughed.
"Ok, so we had this salad, I think pasta salad, with chunks of
veggies in it. We talked a lot while we ate, and Dad stopped
talking and got up and walked around, waving his arms."
Pause.
"Once I understood what was happening, I was paralyzed,
frozen. Mom jumped up, ran toward Dad, and did the
Heimlich on him... it worked fast; I think she only pushed
once or twice and the thing flew out of his mouth like a
missile."
Ty took a breath and exhaled slowly.
"Was that a scary moment for you, Ty?"

"Not while it was happening, but over the days and weeks afterward, it started to sink in and I was pretty freaked out. I started to think I could actually lose my Dad, that an accident can really kill someone you love. I guess I was pretty messed up about it, because I got into some trouble at school. My parents must have understood why I acted out, and they explained that no one was in danger. It made me feel more secure, I guess."

Ty paused, collecting his thoughts. Then he chuckled and said, "Then, we both must have felt the same invisible force because without even talking about it, we just started spending a lot of time together. Sometimes an entire weekend. I was thirteen that summer, so I didn't have a lot going on, so spending time with Dad was pretty cool."

"What kinds of things did you do?"

"Let's see… we camped out in the back yard, we went to the hardware store and fixed stuff around the house, we took bike rides."

"Just the guys?"

"Yeah, Mom didn't seem to mind, she seemed so happy that we were close."

"Well, at that age it's very normal for boys to gravitate away from the mom and towards the male figure in the family."

Ty laughed, "Thanks, Doc, I'm glad I'm at least normal on that count!"

Ron smiled as Ty gathered his backpack and coat to leave.

Chapter 27: October

Ty's parents were in the stands. They had brought a picnic lunch and were enjoying the crisp, sunny day. It was the last home game of the regular season. Their opponent was unfocused, and the Black Bears worked like a well-oiled machine. With less than a minute left, the game was already won. Maine was at its own thirty five yard line. It was second down with five yards to go for a first down. The center snapped the ball to the quarterback. The QB dropped back about five yards while Shawn and Ty ran to their designated areas. The ball was passed and caught by Ty at the first down marker. Ty saw Shawn coming towards him with no opponent nearby. Just for fun, he lateraled the ball to Shawn, where he ran for an additional twenty yards, placing the Bears on their opponent's forty five yard line. With the play over, the two friends gave each other a chest bump by jumping in the air.

Ty had made reservations at the Italian place for that evening. His parents, Tasha and her parents, Shawn, and his dad had all gathered, and the mood was very light-hearted. "You goofs!" Shawn's father said, giving a high give to Ty and Shawn in succession. "You sure know how to entertain!" Ty's father added. Tasha made a point to sit next to Ty's mother to get to know her better. "Ty tells me you're quite an athlete. I'm so glad to hear your shoulder has healed and you're back in the game." Tasha nodded. "Yeah, I was losing hope for a while, then I turned a corner and now I'm as good as new!" Ty's mother asked, "I also heard you want to be a teacher. What age kids do you think you want to work with?" The two of them discussed Tasha's plans for the future, her interests, and, in turn, Tasha learned about Ty's mother's latest hobbies. Normally Tasha's mother would have joined in the conversation, but she could sense that it was best for the two of them to have this time to bond. So instead, she enjoyed holding her husband's hand under the table and listening to the animated sports talk. Everyone had a wonderful time, talking and laughing for hours after the plates were cleared away.

The rest of that month was not relaxing at all for Ty. There seemed to be a practice or a game at every turn, to wrap up the season. He was constantly asked to fill in for his fellow Sports Aid workers, and he also worked four mornings per week in the University sports rehab center. He enjoyed all of it, but any time he had to himself, he just wanted to veg out or hang out with Shawn. He had no energy left for Tasha. He would call her daily but he often begged off getting together. 'I'm just fried,' he would say, and Tasha seemed to patiently understand... but not for long.

Ty truly enjoyed his work at the rehab. He was already used to the gym, since he worked out there often with Shawn. On Halloween morning, Ty arrived for his shift to find some of the students dressed in costumes. He thought it was cute, but he wouldn't be caught dead working in a costume. His first "client" was a sophomore who had recently joined the same pick-up basketball team as Ty. "Hey, Fred." Ty greeted the student with an outstretched hand. "Good to see you, but sorry to hear you torqued your knee." Fred nodded and shook Ty's hand. "I hope you can work some magic on me... I miss the crew." "We'll get you back out there as soon as possible... you always kept me honest on the court." Fred smiled. He was eager to do whatever it took, which made things very easy on Ty. They spent their first session doing wall sits, ab work, and hamstring stretches. His supervisor came by every fifteen minutes or so to give Ty direction or encouragement. When the hour was over, Fred thanked Ty as they both rushed off to their next class.

Chapter 28: November

November began on a negative note. Tasha started to complain to Ty that he was neglecting her, and Ty was getting angry. After a week of arguing over the phone, he decided to confront Tasha in person. He called to ask if he could stop over, and he realized this was the first time he wasn't looking forward to the visit.

Tasha let Ty in without a word. He flopped down on her couch and waited for her to join him. After she used the restroom, she sat on a chair across from him.

"Tash, you know I've been busy the past few weeks. Why are you being so passive aggressive about it?" Tasha's eyes widened and she got angry as well. "Excuse me?" Ty hesitated, then tried to be more diplomatic. "Just because I haven't made much time for us doesn't mean anything."

Tasha was not pleased with that answer. "Well, it means something to me. I know you've had a lot of commitments lately, but whenever you've had a break, you've chosen to spend it with Shawn instead of me." "That's because I was still stressed out. When I'm with Shawn, it's easy, we can blow off steam, like with a workout or a drive." "Why don't you feel the same way about our time together?" Ty thought for a moment. His case was getting flimsier by the second. He wanted to remain angry, to remain indignant, but she had a point. "Tash, I guess you're right. I was being selfish. I wanted easy down time, and I guess I view our time together as a little more serious, like, I have to say the right stuff and give you my full attention. So, when I was busy and fried, I just didn't have the energy." "It sort of sounds like an insult, Ty, but I'm willing to give you another chance if we can come up with a solution." "You want to go to Ron's with me next month?" Tasha hesitated. "I don't know, that's your time. I have a couple ideas if you're willing to hear them." Ty did not hesitate. "Yeah, I do want to hear them. I don't want to lose you, I just can't guarantee I won't be busy or maxed out in the future." "Why don't we take a walk somewhere quiet so we can finish this." "That's a great idea," Ty said. His anger was gone, and he was now able to step inside Tasha's shoes. She must have been feeling neglected, and she was worth more than that.

"Ok," Tasha began, once they were walking a wooded trail. They were not holding hands, like they normally did. "How about if whenever one of us is stressed, they spell it out clearly. I agree that if you are not in the right mood to want to hang out, that's understandable, but I need to see you at least once or twice a week, to know you care and to stay connected. We can have just a short visit, like a meal together, and we'll both know it's not the time for any heavy conversation, and to not place any demands." Ty listened in silence, so Tasha continued. "I do this with my friend Nina all the time... If she needs me to listen, or to be there for her, or to spend time with her but I'm feeling overextended or crabby, I just let her know how I'm feeling so she knows what to expect. Plus, I keep the visit shorter than usual so I don't feel burned out. In the end, I'm always glad we spent the time together. I'm not asking for all your free time, Ty." Ty jumped in. "I know. You've got friends, commitments, too. I love spending time with you, I just have my moods. I didn't mean to say earlier that being with you is work. It's just that I don't want to screw this up, so I want to be at my best when we're together." "We'll figure it out. Let's just keep each other informed, and be honest. As you know, I'll always let you know when it feels like you need to pay more attention to the queen." Ty laughed, then turned to give her a kiss. "You are the queen, no joke! Thanks for keeping me on the payroll." Tasha nodded, "You're worth it."

Chapter 29: December

The first week of December, a letter came in the mail; Tasha was going to New Mexico to volunteer as a substitute gym teacher on a Native American reservation. "It's an opportunity I can't pass up," Tasha said. She had applied months ago and was impatient to hear if she was accepted into the program. "I know, and I'm excited for you. I'm just jealous. Can you sneak me in your carryon bag?" They both laughed, but Ty was not laughing on the inside.

Ty and Ron decided to take a hike in lieu of their normal session. Ty was surprised at the old man's stamina. "You're in pretty good shape, old timer," Ty joked. "I've got a few miles left in me yet... Hey, what are your plans for winter vacation?" Ty sighed, hunching his shoulders. "Tasha's leaving me." "Come again?" Ron asked. Ty clarified. "She's doing an internship for four whole weeks! Shawn's gonna be gone about three weeks with his mom to Puerto Rico, so I'm the odd man out." Ron nodded. "I can see where you'd be disappointed. Can you think of some things you've been wanting to do, but either never had the time, or your partner wasn't interested?" "Not really," Ty answered. "Why don't you give it some thought. Let's try again on our way back down." They hiked in silence for several minutes, enjoying the insulated quiet that the snow had created. "Sure is quiet out here," Ty observed. "I guess I kind of like it." Ron smiled, not feeling the need to add anything. He was pleased to see this young man communing with nature and finding comfort in silence and simplicity. "It's a sign of inner peace, when a person can enjoy the quiet. What do you think?" "I guess so," Ty said, shaking his head. "I barely recognize myself these days!" They both laughed. "Ty, being content and at peace is man's highest goal, or at least one of the hardest things to achieve. You're well on your way, and ahead of the game for most kids your age."

A short while later, as they made their descent, Ty returned to their earlier conversation. "I know… I want to spend some time with Lacy, but not at home. Do you think I could sneak her into the dorm during break?" Ron laughed. "Probably, but now that you mention it, I have a better idea. I'm going away on vacation myself for three weeks. Do you want to house-sit, you and Lacy?" Ty nodded. "That would be cool, thanks, Ron." "Well, you're doing me the favor. But I'm glad you've found something to occupy your time next month. What do you want me to stock the fridge with?" Ty laughed. "No worries, Ron, my mom stuffs me like a turkey over Christmas, so every January, for the first few weeks, I can't even think about food. Lacy and I will go for lots of runs instead." The pair finished the hike and shook on their deal before they parted ways.

Ty felt he did well on his finals and was feeling grateful to have a full day with Tasha before she had to leave. They spent the morning hiking through the woods, then had a snowball fight with her neighbors. After ordering take-out for dinner, Ty found the moment to offer his gift. He held out a small box to her. "Merry Christmas," he said, his voice quieting, "I hope you'll wear this while you're away, to remind you how I feel about you, and that I will be waiting for you when you come back." Tasha smiled, then opened the package. Inside was a gold ring, with a small gemstone. It was simple but good quality. It was actually beautiful in its understated elegance. "Oh, Ty, thank you! It's gorgeous. Of course I'll wear it... all the time!" Ty smiled. "I know it sounds corny, but I'm trying to tell you that I want to be exclusive with you. I mean, of course we haven't been dating other people, but I wanted to make it official. Do you feel the same way?" Tasha leaned in to kiss him. "Let's see if this kiss gives you the answer." For a few short moments, Ty was able to forget about her upcoming trip, and dreading his long winter break without her. He was happy, grateful, and content.

Chapter 30: January

On New Year's Day, Ty's father drove him to Ron's house. Lacy was in the back seat, unaware of the plan to spend more time with Ty. The three of them walked around the yard, which was very spacious and had deep woods beyond the fence line. "Dad, you want to stay for a while and get the kinks out? The woods back there are good for walking, Ron said." His father was surprised by the offer, and replied, "Sure, I'd love to." They had a great time, laughing and talking.

When they returned to the house, Ty made his father a cup of coffee before he drove back home. "You're gonna be ok here all by your lonesome?" Ty's father asked. "You bet. I've actually been looking forward to it." "I'm impressed, Ty. At your age, I would have gone crazy with the thought of being by myself for more than a day or two." Ty smiled. "I guess each generation evolves!" "You got it, son. I have to admit this arrangement does have its appeal. Eat what you want, sleep in as late as you want, no one to nag you...I'm just kidding, your mom doesn't nag me... at least not more than I need." They both laughed. His father rose to put his cup in the sink. "Ok, I will leave you to your Buddhist retreat... enjoy!" They embraced, then Ty lead him out to his car.

As Lacy found the softest carpet in the house to lie on, Ty decided to take a tour of the house. It was open, airy, and filled with plants. There was a media room with a large television, and, in contrast, a spacious yoga room with a bamboo floor and floor to ceiling windows overlooking the woods. "Wow," he said aloud. He was going to get spoiled.

Over the following weeks, Ty spoke with Tasha on the phone every night. After being apart for four days, Ty had gotten his first call. Ty had been warned, so he wasn't upset. With no reliable cell reception, Tasha had to make arrangements to use a land line. "Hey, Ty!" Ty was excited to hear her voice. "Yeah, how's it going Tasha?" "Good, I really like it! The kids are adorable, and my roommate is cool. She's a Math teacher, but really fun, we hang out together after school lets out." "What do you guys do together?" Ty inquired. "We've gone running twice, and we go out for tacos." Ty laughed. "Tacos? Why on earth would you eat tacos in New Mexico?" They both laughed. "I miss you," Ty said. "Me too. I'm having fun and all, but I do miss you. Maybe someday we can come back here, on a vacation. It's absolutely beautiful." "Yeah, let's make a point of it. When we both start making some money." "So, what are you and Lacy doing up in freezing cold Maine?" "Actually, we're running a lot, so the weather isn't really bothering us too much. The snow's not deep in the woods, so we go back there mostly. She's getting up there, so the old girl takes long naps on this shaggy rug after our workouts. She's having a ball." "I'm glad to hear that, Ty. I knew you'd find stuff to do." "Yeah, it was hard to get used to at first, but it's pretty cool now. I'm not just watching tv all day." Tasha laughed. "I believe you, Ty. It sounds like you're making great use of your free time." They talked for several more minutes, then reluctantly said good night.

One evening after having talked with Tasha, Ty found himself gravitating toward Ron's yoga room. He wasn't interested in yoga, but the room pulled him in nonetheless. He padded barefoot on the bamboo floor, feeling a need for quiet reverence; this space seemed somewhat sacred. He looked at and touched the various objects in the room; stone statues of various eastern figures, a metal bowl, and yoga accessories such as mats and cork blocks. The room was uncluttered despite its contents, and he liked that very much. He was used to living in a tiny dorm room, among boxes, his mountain bike, and heaps of dirty laundry and trash. He spread his arms out, enjoying the open space. It was roomy and free, but also felt like a safe cocoon. He wandered over to the large expanse of windows to gaze at the stars. He drank in the quiet, surprising himself. For the remainder of housesitting stint, he made it a regular habit to spend a few moments in this room each night before heading to bed.

By the end of the second week, Ty was counting the days until Shawn came back. He had had his fill of the television, and Lacy seemed to want shorter and shorter runs. She was content chasing squirrels in the back yard and taking long naps. He even had read the two novels for his upcoming class. He had enjoyed being king of the castle. But, despite all this freedom, Ty was ready to get back to his normal life; back among the people, the noise, and the activity of college life.

By the end of January, life did return to normal. Ty and Shawn worked out most afternoons, and Tasha saw Ty every evening she didn't have a game or a practice.

Chapter 31: February

Ty was getting so tired of being a basketball widower to Tasha that he begged Shawn to hang out with him on a gloomy February afternoon. They gorged themselves on pizza and the basketball game on the big screen at their favorite hangout. When the game was over and the tab settled, Shawn said, "Hey, how about getting a little crazy?" Ty raised an eyebrow. "What do you have in mind?" "It involves toilet paper, a stuffed animal, and glow sticks." Ty could barely contain himself. "Dude, I'm in!" They laughed their heads off as they exited the restaurant.

Three hours later, in the dark and the cold, Ty's buzz had been thoroughly killed. "Shawn, she's not coming, can we give it a break?" They had been camping out in front of the dorm room window of Shawn's latest crush. He had wrapped a giant teddy bear in toilet paper and put glow sticks in its ears. The young woman Shawn was interested in was supposed to come home, see the love shrine, and invite Shawn in for some very private time. No dice. She never returned, and the toilet papered bear, that was supposedly a private joke between Romeo and Juliet, was losing all its mummy wrappings. "Damn it, I feel like a tool!" Shawn yelled into the night. "Hey, at least you tried. Let's take a picture and you can send it to her on her phone." "Not a bad idea. I hope the flash on my phone is bright enough." Ty had Shawn pose with the bear as he took the shot. "You really are a tool. A lovesick tool!"

The two best friends picked up the bear, shoved it into the back seat, and headed back to Shawn's room to order yet another pizza. It was going to be a long, depressing night.

"Physical Education Sampler" was a course Ty had enjoyed up to this point, but the next unit was Yoga, and he was NOT in the mood. He was looking forward to it as much as a fifth grade boy would the square dancing unit of gym class. For the next four weeks, Ty was planning on hating this class.
A tall, lanky man, in his late seventies, walked into the center of the studio. Most of the students were surprised at how old he was. Most were expecting a middle aged woman, Mara, who normally taught all the yoga classes at the school.
"I'm Hank," the man said in a calm yet assertive voice. He looked around the room, inviting the students to make eye contact with him. A few did, and Ty noticed Hank smiled warmly back at them. "This is just an introduction to yoga, but I take yoga very seriously, so plan on getting much more than your money's worth."
The students nervously laughed, then the room was quiet again.
Hank explained some basics, had the students try out some poses, and then he asked the students to sit and relax. Ty surmised that he was about to tell his life story, which he did.

"I've been practicing yoga for thirty five years, and teaching for thirty. Yoga saved my life, and it continues to do so. In the service, in Vietnam, I killed several people, including some children. That was my job, to get rid of any threats in our way… adults, kids, who came into our camp with the intent to blow us up, along with themselves. Grenades mostly. When I came back to the states, I didn't know how to be. I was so angry, I pushed everyone away, including my wife. Ironically, it was she who reeled me back in… with a threat, actually. She had turned "hippie" while I was fighting for our country, which felt like a stab in the back at the time, and naturally we divorced a couple years after I got home because I treated her so badly. Back in those days, mothers were expected to have full custody of the children, and so my wife threatened to withhold visitation rights to my daughter unless I enrolled in a yoga class in her hippie community center. This was California, if you haven't already guessed." The class laughed. I went in kicking and screaming, but was determined to see it through, for my kids. The rest… you can pretty much guess, since I'm standing here now still teaching and practicing. Yoga helps you make peace with your feelings, and that paves the way to openness to a full and rich life. You can't really experience life with a wall of anger around you."

The class was quiet, and some of the students were looking at the clock. "Ok, kids, get outta here. See you on Friday." He smiled as the students filed out of the room. The teacher's story was cool, but Ty was not happy; this yoga stuff sure smelled a lot like therapy, and he was already being subjected to that elsewhere. He decided to just power through it because he needed the credits towards his program.

That Friday evening, Ty flopped onto Tasha's couch and turned on the game. Tasha approached him a few minutes later and said, "Ok, you ready?" Ty sighed. "I'm not in the mood, sorry." "What? What's the matter, are you in a bad mood or something?" "No, I just don't feel like going out," Ty pouted. Tasha turned off the television and turned to face Ty. "Well, whatever it is that's bothering you, we should talk about it. Stewing isn't going to help. We could take a walk." Ty disagreed. "Can you leave me be, please? I just want to veg out." "But we have plans tonight, plans I've been looking forward to." Ty was losing his patience. "I don't want to go out, I said." Tasha laughed bitterly, "Well, then I'll go by myself. Lock the house up when you leave." Ty thought she was bluffing; she'd go get a snack from the kitchen, then come back to sit with him to watch the game. At the next commercial, he rose to go look for her in the apartment. "Tash?" No answer. He texted her, and she replied instantly. *I'm not ruining my Friday night just because you want to have a pity party with grumpy for dessert.* Ty texted back, *It can't be much fun by yourself.* Tasha replied, *I have no problem entertaining myself. I plan to enjoy my dinner and the movie.* Ty texted, *Ok, good night. Sorry, Tash,* and flopped back down on the couch.

Chapter 33: April

Ty remembered that his parents were h

eading off to Hawaii for a vacation. He hadn't called them in a while but it was almost midnight, so he sent them an e mail to his mom's account.

Hey, Mom and Dad,
Hope you both are doing good. Please give Lacy a hug for me.
This semester my internship is out in the "real world". Once a
week, I observe in the ER and the other two I'm at a rehab center.
Mostly middle-agers recovering from knee surgery. But once in a
while, they get an athlete in who wants to get back into peak form.
Those are fun. We work out together, then I ice them down. Some
are Iron Man triathaletes.
Hawaii sounds AWESOME. I doubt our team will ever be invited
to play in Hawaii!
Have a great time and remember I'll be slaving away here NOT on
vacation, so send me something great like a live hula dancer, not a
crummy pineapple!
Love, Ty

Tasha's basketball season was finally over. She'd had an excellent comeback with her healed shoulder. They ate at a Thai restaurant to celebrate her victories this season. Tasha had a spicy fish dish, but Ty stuck with his tried and true pad thai, a noodle and tofu dish topped with scallions and peanuts. He was clumsy with chopsticks, so he wielded a knife and fork, American style. "Ty, do you mind if I ask you a personal question?" Ty nodded, although he was unsure where she was going with this. "Well, I'd still like to understand what's behind all the tension between you and your parents." Tasha hesitated. "Do you want to tell me about it?" Ty tugged at his collar. "Not here, not in a restaurant. But soon, ok?" Tasha nodded. "I'm sorry, Ty, I shouldn't have brought it up here. Whenever you're ready."

A few days later, the young couple met at a small park to watch the sunset. It was quiet, very unusual for the beautiful weather. Ty decided he was ready to tell Tasha more about his life. "So, you want to hear more about my family?" Tasha smiled, "Yes, Ty, I would." "The biggest secret I have is that my parents are forcing me to see a shrink. Only you, Shawn, and, of course, my shrink know. They want me to work on my issues, if you know what I mean." Tasha looked at Ty but didn't speak. She felt it was not her place to fill in the blanks. She wanted Ty to clarify, so she waited. "I didn't realize it when I was growing up, but I had a lot of anger. I took it out on my parents. When I started college, they gave me this letter telling me I had to go to therapy once a month if I wanted them to pay for school." Tasha gave a look of surprise, but still remained silent. "It was a crazy time. I couldn't believe it, and I fought it. I tried to get out of it, but they wouldn't budge. Luckily, Ron is a good guy, so I got used to him and even started to kinda like him. Now we sometimes shoot hoops, chug beers, and gorge ourselves on burgers. He even forced me to do punching bag workouts the summer after freshman year!" Tasha laughed, and so did Ty. "I've gotten used to the deal, and we've pretty much mended the fences. I see that my parents want the best for me, and that includes my happiness." Tasha waited a moment, then replied, "Ty, I'm blown away by this, but my first thought is that I agree, your parents love you very much and I guess they needed to use some tough love to get you to help yourself." Nodding, Ty answered, "I knew you'd be on their side!" He playfully chucked her on the chin. She turned to kiss him. "Thank you for sharing this with me... I really mean it." They hugged and kissed again, longer this time.

The next morning, Ty laid his yoga mat out on the floor. This was his last week of the yoga unit, and he was glad. He'd come out of it unscathed. It was a piece of cake. He learned a lot of poses, and was becoming stronger and more flexible. Hank greeted each student by name as each came into sitting position, bowing slightly to the teacher, hands together in prayer position. When everyone was ready to begin, Hank began a short speech. "Our last week together… some of you must be relieved." Some students laughed, nodding, and others shook their heads. "I see a mixed reaction… some of you loved the class, others want it to be over. Well, it's not over yet. We've learned many poses, we've learned how to breathe, and to notice our breathing. But the essence of yoga is to quiet the mind to let the heart tell its story. The heart holds our deepest intentions. These intentions are pure, and they will lead us to fulfillment. Some examples are forgiveness, acceptance, courage. They are pure in that they will always, I repeat always, bring us closer to oneness." Hank saw confusion on some of the students' faces. "'What the hell is oneness and why should I care?' Well, it means we go beyond the illusions of desire, fear, suffering, ego. We accept what the universe has laid out for us, and in turn, we connect in peace with all beings, becoming one. Ok, enough theory, let's get down to it."

Hank stood up to turn on some soft music. "Lie back on your mats, make yourself comfortable. Close your eyes, and just listen to my directions. Let's start with slow, intentional breaths. Let your belly expand, bringing in the fresh air. Hold it for a moment, then let your belly hollow out, expelling the air completely. We will keep that up for fifteen or twenty minutes. The trick is to quiet the mind. I will give you guidance, and sometimes I will be quiet, but your task is to let your mind relax. If you have a thought or you see a mental image, accept it without judgment, but let it pass by, like it's on a conveyor belt. The goal is to gently clear the mind of thoughts."

The students did as they were asked, and to varying degrees of success. Hank could read it on their faces... smiles, relaxed jaws, clenched jaws and grimaces... the whole spectrum. He noticed Ty was doing the most grimacing. When the hour was up, Ty could not get out of there fast enough.

Two days later, Ty was on the mat again. The last yoga class. He was not sad to see this unit end. They repeated the same exercise as earlier in the week, and Ty suffered through it. He felt so angry, like a prisoner in solitary. The silence tortured him, and his thoughts were not pleasant. Memories came up as well, which Ty pushed away in anger as soon as they came up. When class was over and everyone started filing out, Hank approached Ty, and to his horror, Hank addressed him. "Ty, do you have time to stay after class... or can we make an appointment for tomorrow?" Ty looked confused. "Did I do something wrong? Hey, I came to every class, you're going to pass me, right?"
Hank took a deep breath, then looked at Ty, with a warm smile. "Ty, I'm surprised you don't have any broken teeth from this week." Ty looked away, guilty as sin. "I did what I was supposed to, can't you please let it go?" Hank paused, then answered, "I see anger in you, Ty, that is holding you back from living your life; you have a shell of anger around you, and that will prevent even the good things from coming in." Ty was not in the mood. "I already have a shrink, thank you anyways. I'd like to leave now." Hank played his last card. "I need you to spend an hour with me by the end of the week if you want a passing grade in this unit." Ty stood up and stormed out of the room without a response.

On Friday morning, Ty emailed his teacher to set up the appointment. He had cooled off and decided he could survive one more hour with this crackpot. Hank responded a few hours later and directed him to come to the studio at six pm. Ty had his mat rolled out on the floor, and was doing some stretches, when Hank arrived. He got right down to business. "Do everything I say for the next hour, then you are a free man." Ty shrugged. Hank took Ty through the breathing meditations again, and each time Ty grimaced, Hank talked him through it. "Ty, you're doing fine. The fact that you are still here is all that counts. When you have a thought, accept it, and invite it to pass by. When you feel a feeling, accept it. Don't shove it away." More grimacing. "Ty, can you tell me what you are experiencing?"

There was silence, and then Ty said, "This is bullshit." "Ok… not the answer I was hoping for. But that tells me something useful nonetheless. You are resisting. Are you feeling anger?" "Bingo." Ty retorted, sarcasm in his voice. "Breathe, Ty, accept. Each time you feel anger coming, focus back to your breath." Ty tried hard to do as he was instructed, but each time he focused on his breath, and things quieted down, he felt extremely uncomfortable. He felt a mixture of fear and sadness. He felt like a small child. He hated that with a passion. "Let go of your anger, Ty. Let yourself feel the other feelings; it is the only way to get to the other side." "Other side of what?" Ty demanded, losing patience. "Anger is a wall; fear, sadness, shame, they are what the wall is hiding. When you dive into the pool of true feeling, and there are only four true emotions, joy, fear, shame, and sadness, when you dive into those true feelings, it will heal you and lead you to the other side, which is peace and oneness."

After a few more moments, Hank instructed Ty to sit up. Ty's expression was a mixture of exhaustion and annoyance. "Ty, the more you allow yourself that quiet space to feel the true emotions, the sooner you will shed your anger and come to peace." Ty avoided eye contact. He couldn't wait to get out of there. Hank extended his hand, saying, "I hope you will continue the practice, Ty. You can work with me any time you want." Ty nodded, then moved to pack up his things.

Chapter 34: May

"Ty, I want to talk about your birth mother."
Pause.
"I don't remember her. She died when I was a baby, then I got adopted."
"Can we explore something?"
"I guess."
"Parents that can't take care of themselves, can't truly take care of their children, even if they feel tremendous love for them. Their problems, their pain, take away their strength."
"You're saying that my mom used drugs to deal with her pain."
"I would venture a guess that she was neglected and abused in her childhood much like you were under her care. She probably felt a pain that could be temporarily dulled with drugs or alcohol. She didn't know how to get healthier forms of help."
"So I'm supposed to feel sorry for her."
"Not pity, but could we work on understanding, acceptance?"
Ty said nothing, but looked Ron calmly in the eyes.
"I'll take that as an 'I suppose...'"
They both laughed, despite the tension.
"Since I know you've come to love and trust me implicitly, I'm asking you FOR THE FIRST TIME FOR THE RECORD to close your eyes."
Ty closed his eyes while raising his eyebrows.
"The goal here is to clear your mind. First, concentrate on your breathing, and nothing else. Let's do about three minutes."
Three minutes elapsed.
"Is your mind clear?"
"No, Ron," Ty said, with resentment in his voice. "I almost failed my yoga class because of it! Plus, you made me do this a few years ago... you're trotting out old material on me?"

Ron thought for a moment. "A calm mind takes work, practice, time. All you need is the desire, and it will eventually start to happen. Let's do a little more… next step is to breathe in deeply for five counts, pause for one count, then slowly exhale for at least seven counts. Let your belly expand on the inhalation, and suck in that damned six pack of yours on the exhalation. Keep your mind clear."

Ty did the exercise for about three minutes more, then opened his eyes.

"Is that it?"

"Yes, for now. I hope you can commit to doing that a few times each day, and in a month or two we'll look to see if you're any closer to a calm mind and acceptance."

Ty rolled his eyes, got up to leave, and patted Ron on the back on his way out.

Ty entered Tasha's kitchen and threw his gym bag into a corner. "TASHA?" Pause. "Are you here?"

A muffled call from the bathroom, shower running, "I'll be out in a sec."

In the meantime, Ty went to the sink for a glass of water, still shaking his head and fuming from his anger at what had just happened during his shift at the rehab center.

In his impatience, Ty started pacing the room. That got boring, so he washed a few dishes.

"You almost done?" Ty called again.

No reply.

A few moments later, Tasha appeared in a robe and a towel wrapped around her head.

"What's the matter? You totally disturbed my relaxing shower."

"Well, 'scuse me!" Ty gave a sigh of exasperation. "I'm so pissed at my boss, I want to break something!"

"Calm down and tell me what happened."

"She accused me of scaring away one of the clients. She said she quit because it was too hard. How the hell do these people expect to get better if someone doesn't push them? That lady, Mrs. Zink, I swear, she's gonna have rotator cuff pain for the rest of her life if she doesn't strengthen her muscles. What are they running over there, a rehab or a SPA?" Ty pounded the counter with his fist.

"That really sucks, Ty. But you have to play by their rules."

"Screw their rules!"

"Why don't you sleep on it. Promise you didn't burn a bridge over there."

"No, I just left at the end of my shift. I didn't argue with her, but I certainly didn't apologize!"

"Come here, I didn't even get a kiss yet."

Ty rubbed his hands over his face. "I'm too worked up. I'm gonna go for a run or something."

Tasha had a look of disappointment on her face, but then she had a change of heart. "That sounds like a good plan, Ty. Come by later if you feel like it."

Ty pecked her on the cheek and left.

Two hours later, he called Tasha and made plans to come back to her apartment. When he walked in the door, he still looked upset.

"The run didn't help. I'm still mad!"

"Well, crabby crank, I'm not going to spend my Friday afternoon like this. Either you let me give you a nice big hug, or you go somewhere else to stew."

Ty looked offended. "That's pretty 'fair weather friend' of you."

"Ty, I just mean you need some time to cool down. You won't be this upset forever. You can still find a way to enjoy your internship and succeed there. The lady was probably a complainer by nature."

Ty sighed and looked into Tasha's eyes. "I'm ready for my hug."

Tasha smiled and opened her arms wide. They embraced for several minutes, Ty enjoying the warmth and comfort of her breathing.

"You hungry?" he asked.

"Not really…" Tasha said, drawing out the last word.

Ty laughed, kissed her deeply, and picked her up, heading for the staircase.

After they had made love, Ty stroked Tasha's hair. They stayed like that for a long time.

"Tell me why you love me," Tasha teased.

Ty answered quickly.

"Because you're hot."

Tasha laughed. "Be serious."

"Okay. You talk me off the ledge. Your hugs tame me. Your lips taste TASTY! I'm so proud to be seen with you in public. I'm proud of your talents, your hard work. Your skin is so silky…" Ty's voice trailed off as he proceeded to kiss Tasha's shoulder, caressing her arm.

A small tear leaked out of Tasha's right eye. Ty did not notice it.

She rolled onto her back to better look at this young man.

"You're beautiful, Ty. Your eyes, your nose…"

She looked at him intently, stroking his cheek.

"You love me?" Ty asked.

Tasha smiled, and another tear leaked out.

She nodded.

Ty found the tear and kissed it.

They both smiled.

Tasha closed her eyes.

A few minutes passed, then Tasha opened her eyes and stretched up her arms.

"Let's cook!"

She grabbed Ty's hand and they got up to get dressed, then headed downstairs.

"What's on the menu, I'm starved." Ty's voice was bright.

"Meatballs and roasted red pepper sauce."

"Sounds good!" He kissed her neck. "How am I going to concentrate on my work, chef?"

Tasha laughed.

"Then I guess you're not hungry, we can skip it."

Ty's face showed shock.

"Ok, boss, sorry, I'm at your beck and call!" He made a salute in Tasha's direction.

"First, some tunes, then, wash your paws."

Ty did as he was told. The haunting, romantic voices of the Gypsy Kings reverberated around the room.

"Excellent choice," she said. "I need you to wash and pierce a hole in each pepper, then lay them on a cookie sheet."

Tasha started on the meatballs.

Every so often, Ty stole a kiss. Tasha didn't protest. They both felt peaceful and happy.

For a few minutes, they worked in silence, each concentrating on their own task.

Ty turned to her. "I like this. Just being with you. Cooking."

"Yeah. Me too. Now, Private, time to put those in the broiler. Let them get charred, then turn off the heat and let them sit in the oven for about fifteen."

Another mock salute, and Ty got down to business.

Tasha was rubbing dried oregano and basil between her palms, letting the fragrant powder fall into the meat mixture.

"Start the wok with some olive oil for me."

Again, Ty complied. "It's startin' to smell GOOD in here!"

They both smiled. Tasha sang to the music.

As she put the meatballs on a broiler pan, she called to her helper.

"Can you boil a pot of water for the spaghetti?"

Another salute and Ty started to look for the pot.

Thirty minutes later, they sat down with plates of steaming hot food.

"Smells awesome!" Ty said, ready to dig in.

At first they ate in comfortable silence, then when his plate was half empty, he turned to Tasha.

"Tell me something about your life, your past, that I don't know already."

"Okay, let me come up with a memory."

After a pause, Tasha continued.

"I was about eight years old. My neighbor Dane and I were in our yard playing like usual, but this time he showed up with a magnifying glass, looking really excited. It was a fall day, with dry leaves all over the grass, and he showed me how to use the sun to burn a hole in the leaves. It was really cool... Until my mom caught us."

Ty nodded his head. "Yeah, parents, the perpetual kill-joys." They both laughed.

"So, my mom came running out of the house, asking us what the heck we were doing. When it registered in her head, she really started to freak out. She yelled at Dane to stop it and yelled some more, telling him to go home and never come back with that magnifying glass."

Tasha took a drink of her water.

"After he was gone, I thought I was going to get it, but instead my mom just sat on the back steps and cried, her shoulders shaking. I considered getting as far away from her as possible, but I realized I wasn't in trouble and I decided I would try to comfort her. When she calmed down enough to talk, she explained that she didn't think Dane was a bad kid. But what we were doing with the leaves reminded her of a very painful experience in her life. When she was about my age, she started to explain, her family home had caught fire in the night. Everyone in the family made it out safely, but not her dog. When everyone was outside the burning house, she begged her father to let her go back in to find their pet. He refused to let her go. Needless to say, the dog died in the fire."

"Oh my God," Ty said, his eyes cast down, staring at his plate.

"She's never forgiven herself."

"Why? She tried to save him!"

"She still feels bad because she believes she should have remembered to grab him on her way out. People have a bad habit of blaming themselves when there is no one to blame."

"That sucks. Your mom is so sweet, she wouldn't hurt a fly."

"Maybe that's why she still feels bad."

Ty reached out to hold Tasha's hand while they finished their meal.

"Tash, you think I need to apologize to my boss?"

"An apology, maybe, but you should talk to her at least. What do you think she would want to hear?"

Ty sat for a minute, running his finger over one of Tasha's rings.

"I could promise to not do it again. Not lecture the clients."

"That sounds great, Ty, and, how about bringing it to your boss' attention next time it comes up, so she can guide you as to how she wants you to manage the situation. You're still an intern, you know. Interns are there to learn, not solve everything."

"I'll give it a try. Seriously, I wasn't rude to Mrs. Zink, I just kept reminding her."

"Well, they would have to close their doors if they didn't accommodate the clients' quirks."

"Yeah, people can be a pain in the ass."

They both laughed.

Ty's face went serious and he looked her in the eyes.

"I love you. You're so good to me."

"You're worth it, babe."

They enjoyed a long kiss.

After they finished washing the dishes, Tasha turned off the music and brought them back to reality.

"I've got to leave in ten, my study group meets tonight."

"Yeah, all good things must come to an end," Ty said glumly.

"I suppose I should study, too. Gotta keep up with your standards!"

They both laughed.

They gave each other a kiss and a long hug, and Ty was out the door.

Chapter 35: June

Ty had the day off, but Tasha and Shawn were both busy, so he decided to take a hike by himself. He took a bus to a nearby town and walked a half mile to a hiking trail. It was ten am, a little muggy from last night's rain. As he started up the trail, littered with scrub pines and pink granite boulders, his mind filled. He thought about his parents, how they were trying to get him to change, and it no longer angered him. He remembered the time his mom fell on the floor, crying. She had been yelling at him. He was probably ten years old at the time. He pictured her slowly calming down, then out of the blue she started in on her yoga poses. One minute she was screaming and crying, the next she was doing downward dogs and warrior two's with such strength and focus, it caught his attention. He realized now that she was coping. She had lost her cool with him and so she turned it around. He wondered what he had done to make her so upset. He never was very aware of what he did wrong. His parents talked to him a lot, but whenever it felt like a critique he made his ears go deaf. As a young adult now, he realized his mom was a survivor, and a warrior. He supposed he needed to start following her ways. He felt very proud of her, glad she was his mom after all. She never kicked him out of the house. He imagined if a kid made a parent crazy, they'd be tempted to give them back... back to the hospital where they were born, or back to the judge if they were adopted. He took a moment to savor the fact that his mom had stuck it out.
He then felt an intense sadness. It washed over him, and he felt very alone. He stopped in his tracks and tried some deep breathing. It wasn't helping much. "Goddamned bastard Hank," Ty muttered to himself. Two weeks ago, he had decided to take the teacher up on his offer, and they had been working together three times a week... lots of annoying feelings were coming up in Ty, but he didn't resist it as much as before.

He brought himself back to the present, and resumed his hike. He quickly reached the summit, looked over the valley of pines and country roads, then found a rock to sit on. He closed his eyes, and started noticing his breathing. Four in, belly expands, five out, belly caves in. Whenever his mind wandered to other subjects, he turned his attention back to his breath. He noticed the fresh air, a slight breeze on his face, a chicadee's chirp. It was so peaceful on the mountain. He felt grateful to be alive. He didn't feel the fear anymore. No anger at that moment. That surprised him, and then it didn't. He had Tasha, he had Shawn, he had parents who believed in him. "Wow," he said aloud. A light bulb had gone off. He returned to his breathing for another set of nine inhalations and exhalations. He then heard the distant voices of other hikers and decided his session was done. Well done. He felt at peace and alive.

Ty strolled into Ron's office a few minutes early, which gave Ron quite a shock. After he wiped the smile off his face, he asked Ty, "So...have you been doing your breathing several times a day?"
"Yes, Zen Master. Up to my eyeballs in meditating sessions!"
 "Ok, next month we'll talk about it. So, what are you summer plans?"
"Another sweet deal. I seem to have the touch!"
"Do tell."
"My internship at the rehab center has turned into a... drum roll, please... paying summer job!"
"Congratulations, Ty. They must be pleased with your work."
"Yes, I am pretty popular there. Even if we have to coddle the clients, it's a great opportunity."
Ron rolled his eyes, smiling.

"Are you still doing your focused breathing?" Ron asked.
"Yeah, Tasha caught me doing it once and now she's my meditation buddy!"
"Adorable. She's a keeper."
"It really puts her in the mood, if you know what I mean, Doc."
Ron covered his ears and shook his head side to side dramatically.
"BAH BAH BAH BAH BAH! I CAN'T HEAR YOU!!!"
They both laughed.
"What did you tell her about it? Meaning, why you're doing it?"
"I told her it's to help me accept my past. The good, the bad, and the ugly."
"Yes, young Skywalker."
Ty rolled his eyes, but smiled in spite of himself.
"I like doing it with her … every time I see her we take five minutes out."
"Again, awesome. You're very evolved, you know."
"Yeah, thanks to you, I'm a sensitive pansy!"
"Whatever. You'll thank me later. Please close your eyes and I have a question…Can you forgive your birth mom?"
"Uh, I guess so."
"Feelings? Reaction?"
"I can let it go?"
"Excellent start… keep going."
"She can have peace. People that die need peace. If you forgive them, they can have peace. My dad always talks like that when someone we know dies."
"Do you believe it?"
"Yes."
"Do you think you can do that for your birth mom?"
"Yes, but how?"

"By continuing to meditate. It will come. If you have the intention of forgiving your mom, it will happen. Next question, can you wish her peace? She is dead, after all."

"I think so."

"If you forgive her and wish her peace, what do you think that will do for you?"

"I'll be a more evolved person, to use your words."

"Simpler answer, please."

"Ok, ok. I will have peace."

"Yes. More rewards… what about self esteem?"

"A mature person forgives."

"I'm sorry, let me back up a bit. When you accept and forgive what happened to you, can you still hold on to the feeling that you weren't good enough, not special enough to make your mom want to clean up her act and take better care of you?"

"I guess."

"I promise you this will come with your meditation. If you continue to wish her peace, it will all take care of itself."

"I think my self-esteem is pretty high, if I do say so myself."

"I don't mean outward manifestations of self-esteem, but an unconscious capacity for self-love and inner peace."

"Very zen."

"I highly doubt, when you were living with your parents from age three to eighteen, that you had much self-love or inner peace."

"You would probably be right. Although I didn't realize it."

"Exactly. You were a friendly, intelligent, giving, popular young man. But someone felt your angst… you unconsciously saw to that. Who was it?"

Silence.

"Mom."

"Yes. I'm not bringing this up to make you feel guilty. I'm just trying to show you how the brain and the heart work... Your response was biological, natural. Most adopted kids have the same response as you did, to use the mother figure as a punching bag when she was not the one who caused you the pain. I'm sure you remember with fondness your forced photo-op training sessions the summer you worked at the resort..."

"Loved every sweaty minute of it!"

"I've seen you find some very productive outlets for your anger; it no longer has power over you. Would you agree?"

"Definitely. When I was a kid, my mother dragged me to about five different therapists to try to deal with this exact stuff. But I blew it off."

"That's ok, Ty. What's important now is that you want to heal, you're ready now. You want peace, you want to be happy."

"And my mom?"

Ron replied with a question, "What do you think she wants most in the world?"

"To see me evolve."

"More specifically..."

"That I'm not mad at the world anymore. I can enjoy life, that kind of stuff."

"YES! I have to tell you, Ty. I am getting as much out of these sessions as you are."

"Awww, gee willikers."

"Bite me."

They both laughed.

"And, one more thing about anger. Anger is a response, not a true feeling, a distraction from the pain underneath. Tell me about a close friend you've had who was mad for a long time."

"Well, I've had friends who've been dumped and they stay so mad, that they end up being mad at all other girls. But they spend a lot of time complaining that they don't have a girlfriend. They don't see the connection."

"When your buddy is mad, even months after the breakup, would you say that his pain has healed?"

"No."

"Would you say he allowed himself to feel his sadness, his hurt?"

"I get it. The anger is a cover up for the hurt. The pain is too uncomfortable to face because guys don't know how to deal with sadness. They'd rather look tough than weak."

"Would you rather be a tough guy with no love in your life, or a sensitive guy who is in touch with his feelings and has a hot momma by his side?"

Ty looked at Ron, then bent over, laughing.

SENIOR YEAR

"Fourth card. Last card."
Ty took the index card out of Ron's hand. He held it for a minute before looking at it.
"Old Blue."
He smiled. His eyes started to shine with tears, and then he blinked them dry.
Then, he bent his head, put his face in his hands.
Ron but a hand on his shoulder.
A few minutes passed. Ty got up to blow his nose.
Ron gave him a reassuring look. He tried to lighten the mood.
"Come on, Richie Rich. Sounds like a good story is about to unfold before my very ears."
"Cornball."
"That's Mr. Dinosaur Cornball to you. I believe I scored more than you last time we were at the gym."
"Whatever."
Pause.
"Ok. Old Blue was the name we gave my first car. It was an '02 Subaru wagon. Very earthy crunchy, very embarrassing. My parents thought it was cool, and that annoyed me like crazy. I earned Old Blue with my own hard labor. My parents didn't contribute a penny toward the car or the insurance. So that I'd really appreciate it and take good care of it and all that kind of parenting drivel. They turned out to be right. Old Blue was the bomb. It was all mine, no one gave it to me."
Pause.
"My dad and I spent a lot of time fixing it up. Those were good times. I actually discovered my father knew a thing or two. He seemed cool that summer. We took our time, we actually put in a whole new engine. I learned a lot."
Pause.
"I wouldn't have gotten those great times with my dad if they had bought me a car that actually ran."

Both laughed.

"Any road adventures in Blue?"

"The usual. Fender benders, didn't have to repair the body since it was already a junker; that was cool. Smoked my first joint in Blue, did some other things in there, too."

Smile.

"Then some tool stole it. I think it was someone on the team but I wasn't sure and I didn't want to be a geek and get all, 'poor me' and secret detective, so I let it go."

"That sucks. Did you get another car after that?"

"Yes."

Ty shook his head and smiled a bit. "Let's just say, I got it unconventionally."

"You stole it?"

"No, sorry to disappoint you, it's much more boy scout than that. Our neighbor, Mr. Little, he was an old guy. He loved my family, and always gave me and my mom stuff. Food, birthday presents, even hugs, but I dodged those most of the time. He lived by himself, his wife died before I was even born, I think. He was lonely, but cool. After I lost Old Blue, he called me over to ask where my car had gone. I told him, and he asked me to come inside the house. I followed him and he gave me a soda like he always did. He said his doctor said he couldn't drive anymore, so I could borrow the car any time I wanted, as long as I promised not to crash it."

"Just like that? No other strings?"

"No. Just like that. I was stoked. I kept thanking him, saying I'd take great care of it."

Ty sighed dramatically.

"When my mother got wind of the deal, she wasn't happy. She asked me about it, and she said she wasn't going to allow it unless I sit down and listen to what she and Dad had to say. I said something to the effect of 'screw you' and stormed out. I drove off in his car, and got a speeding ticket… and, remember, my name wasn't on the registration papers. When the cops questioned my mother, she handed me a note saying something like, 'I'll only back you up if you agree in advance to all our conditions'. I said, 'yeah', and so I just got a small fine and community service. I tried to leave without being subjected to their lecture, but my dad blocked the door and I sat down at the table. My mother handed me another note and they both went out to take a walk. It said something like, 'If you want to continue to have the privilege of borrowing Mr. Little's car, then you will agree to spend forty-five minutes with him every day until further notice.' That was it. Nothing else. It sounded like a drag, but I was expecting a lot more grief than that, so when they got back they found my note saying 'OK'."

Ty stretched.

"Mr. Little wasn't just getting old, he was dying. I asked him why people came to his house every day and he said he was on hospice." Ty was quiet for a moment, then he began again. "He had cancer."

"No one moved in to take care of him around the clock?"

"Not until six or seven months after I started borrowing the car. Hospice came in the mornings, and I would come around seven at night. I guess you could say I got him ready for bed. I helped him with his meds, rubbed his feet, that kind of thing. After a while, I didn't resent it any more. He was cool, he told cool stories about growing up. He was a wrestler, and even did semi pro for a while, on the side. He loved animals, just like me, and he showed me pictures of all the dogs he'd had. He even had a German Shepherd that saved his son's life. He came running over to Mrs. Little and led her into the kitchen where their son was choking."

Pause.

"When he got really sick, he stayed in his rented hospital bed twenty-four-seven. It was depressing and it stunk in the room, but he still had more stories to tell. Sometimes I stayed four hours. Sometimes I stayed after he fell asleep, even with the hospice people there. The week everyone said he was dying, I took off. After about twenty messages, I finally returned one of my mom's calls and she said he was going to die any hour now. I made it before he died. He wasn't awake; he wasn't going to wake up ever again."

Ty sat there for a long time, just breathing, eyes closed. Some ragged breaths.

"He was cool. I'm glad I got to do that."

Pause.

"My crazy mom."

"Yes, Ty."

Chapter 38 September

Ty walked into Ron's office with a look of mischief on his face. Without even a hello, he proceeded to address Ron.
"I want you to know I blame you for turning me into a PANSY WOOS."
"Come again?"
"I've signed up for TWO, count 'em, TWO yoga classes this semester!"
"That's good news. Yoda is pleased you are not fighting your spiritual work."
"I can't even make you feel even a little bit guilty that you've taken away my manhood?"
"I don't buy that for a second."
"You never were a pushover. That's what's so frustrating about you, I can never get a rise out of you."
"I prefer to call myself extremely interesting because I always offer people a challenge."
"Whatever. Anyways, I will be the bigger person and admit the classes are part of my major."
Ron sat in silence, gloating and beaming.
"At my job, we incorporate yoga into the early stages of rehab. It'll be great to really know what I'm doing, instead of just staying at the surface."
Ron leaned back, eyes wide.
"Ty, you have found your calling. Really, most people don't ever find it. Or, in my case, I invested in two full-blown careers before I finally found my true path."
"Ron, you are a born shrink."
"I'll choose to take that as a very warm compliment."
They laughed.

Ty had heard that Mara's yoga class would give him six pack abs. That would motivate him to give the class his all. He walked into the studio, his fifth session with this teacher. Mara was welcoming and warm, but she got down to business in short order. "Good morning, everyone stand. Mountain pose… focus on your breath, ground your feet into the earth. Lift your toes, settle them back down, strong. Breathe in…. out. Crown of the head reaches up to the sky. Navel in, spine straight, arms straight, shoulders down, let the shoulder blades glide behind your back and down. Breathe. Strong. Arms up, slight back bend, look up to the sky, deep inhale. Arms out, bending down, forward fold. Exhale it all out. Gently sway your head from side to side, relax. Breathe…" Ty knew this easy warmup was nothing like what was to come. He was glad he had gotten a good night's sleep; he was in for quite the workout.

For the next forty minutes, Mara's directives were clear and swift; no time for rest. "Warrior one, warrior two, exalted warrior, back to warrior two, side angle, windmill arms over to plank, chaturanga, updog, down dog…" The rumors about Mara's effect on the students' muscles was no exaggeration. Ty was feeling the pain, and the results.

Mara's voice pulled him out of his thoughts. "Ok, team, dolphins… my favorite!" Ty groaned. The hard work was almost complete. The last ten minutes of class were reserved for savasana, the restful, meditative pose that Ty used to loathe; now he did it with ease. His exhaustion from the workout helped him relax and calm his mind.

On a Sunday afternoon, Tasha suggested they go to a grassy park along the Stillwater River. As usual they each brought picnic foods and settled in for a lazy few hours. They studied and daydreamed for a while, then Ty made a pillow for Tasha's head out of his lap, and he stroked her face. "Can we bottle this moment?" Tasha asked. Ty nodded, as nothing more needed to be said. He was in love, he was relaxed, and for now, neither had a care in the world.

Chapter 39: October

After Ty filled Ron in on the latest details about his upcoming game, they got down to business.

"I'd like you to tell me about your first day at school, freshman year. Your parents dropped you off, right?"

Ty collected his thoughts and began. "Yeah, they drove me here, and my mom kept following me around like she didn't want to let me go. I was rude to her on the last day I saw her, for god's sake. It was just my habit. I never got rid of it. When they were helping me bring my stuff up to the dorm room on the first day, I was giving her crap. Saying that *she* forgot to bring the sheets, that she was embarrassing me by acting all excited about college. When she went to give me a hug goodbye, I turned away instead. Then, they just left. We had plans to go out for pizza before they drove back home but they just left."

"Ok, Ty, now you're twenty one. Talk to me about that first day at college from your twenty one year old brain, your twenty one year old soul. Dig into this."

"I was nervous. I didn't know my roommate, I was nervous about the team. I was not the usual calm, cool, collected stud you've come to know."

They both laughed.

"I dumped my stress on my mother. I hurt her feelings."

Pause.

"Would you say that she cooked up this therapy deal in response to the argument over the sheets?"

Pause.

"No. She's a planner. Not very spontaneous."

"Ty, why do you think she and your father decided to do this, to put you through this?"

"To teach me a lesson."

"What kind of lesson?"

"That you can't treat people like crap and expect to get away with it forever."

"Anything else?"

"I don't know. I came up with a pretty adult answer, you have to admit."

"Yes, but I'd like to come back to this again later, to build upon it."

Ty decided to lighten the mood. "Hey, do you remember me talking about my buddy Mac who plays wheelchair rugby?"

"I think so," Ron replied, curious.

"For his senior thesis he is leading a one credit mini course and he's DESPERATE for people to sign up. He needs fifteen to make it go, so I volunteered."

"What is the course about?"

"Psychology of trauma. I think he's going to talk about his war experiences and stuff. You know, I think when I'm a full-fledged P.T., I might want to work with vets full time."

"Sounds great, Ty. Your interests and training are really coming together... Most students barely know what they want to do upon graduation, and you are well on your way to an enriching career."

Ty smiled, "Aw, gee, don't go all flattering me and all!"

Ron chucked Ty on the arm and they ended the session.

Chapter 40: November

Ty sat in the front row of the lecture hall as usual, in support of Mac. Sometimes Mac would give Ty the signal to dim the lights or turn them back up as he controlled the projector.

As Ty expected, Mac did spend the first third of the course talking about Post Traumatic Stress Disorder, PTSD, and used his military experiences as rich examples of the toll the rigors of war take on the psyche. Today was the start of a new topic, childhood trauma. When the students were seated, quiet and focused, Mac began. "Good morning, sunshines!"

The class groaned but kept their eyes focused on Mac; he was a very engaging speaker. Most of the students were social work majors and had been looking for such a course offering. They were grateful for the opportunity.

Mac continued. "For anyone who still has the syllabus, you know that today we start our second unit, childhood trauma. Raise your hand if you think a four year old can be walking around with PTSD."

Not a single hand went up. "Don't worry, you are in the majority. I'm here to turn that belief on its head. Kids who were the victims of repeated abuse or saw frequent abuse in their home often suffer from PTSD. As we explore our second topic of attachment disorder, keep that in the back of your minds. When we complete this unit, you will all agree that PTSD is not just reserved for those who have seen military action."

The room was quiet as Mac gathered his thoughts.

"Picture if you will, an infant or a child who is abused, neglected, or abandoned. They develop a lot of coping strategies, even survival strategies. For example, let's say your mom is always getting stoned or looking for something to get her stoned. No time for such trivialities as food. What might a four year old do to survive?"

A few tentative hands went in the air. One student suggested the child would rummage around in the cabinets and find their own food. Another offered going out into the world and begging or hustling for food.

"Excellent," said Mac. "Now, given just this one example of doing what has to be done to eat, what are the effects on the child-parent dynamic?"

Ty raised his hand. "Well, the kid doesn't need an adult to get food anymore."

Mac nodded in agreement. "Just imagine, a four year old not dependent on his or her parents. I have to admit I grew up in a caring and functional family, so that blows my mind. But that's the child's reality. Now, let's add abuse to the neglect. The child gets hurt when the parent can't get access to drugs or alcohol. The child never knows when this will occur. Give me some survival strategies."

The class became very engaged and less formal. Students in turn called their answers out instead of raising their hands.

"Hiding." "Disassociation." "Seeking out other parent figures like a teacher."

Mac was pleased. "Yes… and where is the parent-child dynamic now?"

"No trust." "There is no parenting."

"Exactly," replied Mac. The trust is GONE. Parents are no longer gods in the kid's eyes. They are not to be trusted. Don't be fooled, though, humans are hard wired to desire bonding with one's biological parents, and so this fractured state is exceptionally damaging to the fragile child, his view of the world and of himself. That's where shame comes in. Shame is literally the belief that we are not good enough because no one wants to take care of us. The events that caused the shame could be far in the past, but shame grows if it is not healed." Mac took a sip of water and a pause. "Wouldn't you feel worthless if you were treated like a piece of trash?"

The class was silent.

"Now, let's envision this child finally gets removed from the home by social services. He is scared and misses his mom, regardless of what she did to him. He doesn't understand why he was separated from her. As you know, children are extremely ego centric, and so he automatically assumes he did something bad to get kicked out of his home. No one can tell him differently. He eventually gets adopted by a patient and loving family. He is told that this family will never, ever abandon him. You may all think to yourselves, 'good, now he can be healed and happy'." Mac raised his voice for dramatic effect. "WRONG! It is only after he is convinced that he is in a forever family that he can let down his guard. Stop the honeymoon period. We've seen again and again that it is not until the adoption is final or close to being finalized that a child may then feel comfortable enough to present with what we now call reactive attachment disorder, thanks to the pioneer of the field, Foster Cline. This condition, known as RAD, is caused by a breakdown in the normal nurturing and parenting process. Neglect or abuse, whatever happened, the child didn't form trust. HOW COULD HE?!? There was never any guarantee his needs would be met. Most kids that have RAD can't bond with or trust their adoptive parent, even if they're wonderful people. They want to be the boss because they're TOTALLY SCARED OF LOSING CONTROL. Remember the survival strategies we talked about."

The room was quiet, and then one student raised her hand. "In my internship I work with an adoptive parents support group. I've heard several parents say that their child often seems to forget that they're no longer with the abusive parent. They still react, behave, and cope in the same ways."

"Yes," said Mac, "Kids are not very articulate about their thoughts and feelings, so much of their angst gets played out in behaviors and interpersonal dynamics. Children who suffer from RAD keep their coat of armor on when it is no longer needed. It's like putting on a fur coat in the winter, but then never taking it off, even in the heat of the summer. Their PTSD led to developmental trauma; ways of interpreting and reacting that are self-defeating because their brain did not develop in the desired environment of loving care from a parent. Self protection is their soul's focus, and it is self-defeating. Talk to me about this."

Another student volunteered. "They can't get close to their parents, they can't heal, they can't enjoy the love and peace their new family offers."

"Wow, you all are on fire today," Mac answered. "We have to end it here. When we continue next time, we'll explore the pathways to healing, so do not despair!" He gave a smile and the students took their cue to leave. As Ty got up to unhook some cords and wires for Mac so he could pack up his laptop, he saw Mac approach him. "Pretty heavy stuff, hey?" Mac offered.

Ty nodded, but didn't return Mac's gaze. He focused on his task instead.

"Ty, you've told me a little bit about your past. Does this stuff make you uncomfortable?"

Ty decided he couldn't hide from this conversation anymore. "Yes, it's hard to hear this stuff. And it's new to me, so just give me time to absorb it. It's kind of freaking me out right now."

Mac put his hand on Ty's shoulder. "You can always talk to me. And, until your ready, I won't press you."

Ty gave a quick look in Mac's direction and said, "Ok, I gotta go."

No one was more surprised than Ty by how much he came to love yoga. He had only three weeks left of his two yoga courses and was sad to see them come to an end. He enjoyed Mara's class, but it was Hank who was helping him grow. He not only learned some killer poses, his mind became more and more quiet and peaceful. After one especially challenging round of poses, Ty looked forward to savasana, a laying down relaxation at the end of the class time, geared toward both absorbing the benefits of the physical practice they had just done, but also to quiet the mind. On this particular day, Ty noticed that his thoughts were not intrusive, and he could send them on their way with ease. With no distractions, he felt calm and peaceful... The anger and the underlying feelings were gone. Not gone completely from his every day existence, but nowhere to be found at the end of this intense practice session. He felt very grateful and hopeful.

Hank caught a glimpse of Ty smiling. It warmed the old man's soul. He couldn't resist asking Ty to stay to chat after class. "I always have time for you, Hank, you're my man!" Ty joked with Hank, but he truly meant it. Hank had become a friend. "Ty, I want to say how thrilled I am to see you finding peace, and enjoying your practice." Ty nodded in agreement. Then, he laughed, "Who would've thunk it, I fought you so damn hard at first!" "I'm proud of you, son. Are you happy? Do you believe yoga has helped you find peace?" Ty nodded again. "Yeah, I'm in a real good place right now, and I know enough to be grateful, and notice all the good things in my life. I couldn't do that a few short years ago." Hank slapped Ty on the back. "Don't be a stranger after this class is over; I want you to come and co-teach any time you want." Ty was touched. "I'd like that, Hank."

Chapter 41: December

On the last day of Mac's course, the students each gave ten-minute presentations highlighting the most meaningful thing they had learned in the course and what questions they still needed to explore. Ty chose yoga and its healing powers for those with PTSD. When it was his turn to speak, he approached the podium with electrified nerves and slightly shaking hands. He didn't know why he was so worked up, and he couldn't wait until the next five minutes were behind him. He cleared his throat and began.

"Some of you know I'm a Physical Therapy major, not Psych or Social Work like you guys. But there has been a shift in my field to a holistic mind and body approach. Gone are the days when someone comes in to work a knee and all we work on is the knee. First, the whole body's interconnectedness is examined, and a regimen is prescribed that helps the body heal and work as a whole. Many in the PT field now also believe that the spirit and body are closely connected. Emotional stress affects the body in serious ways. Attitude, outlook, habits of decompressing and self care are strong predictors of success in a physical therapy treatment process. I integrate yoga into each client's treatment plan, mainly focused breathing and mindful meditation to address this new trend in the field, which I think is here to stay."

Ty's nerves were calmed down and he felt he was on a roll. He was happy to see a fellow student raise her hand.

"Ty, where do you find the time working with therapy clients to do it all? It's the same in social work, there are so many great approaches to try, but we are only given so much time to work with each client."

Ty nodded his head in agreement. "I hear you, Maggie. But, since I strongly believe in the mind-body connection, I can't let one of the pieces go. It's crucial to success, a lasting healing for the client, so the time spent working on the spirit is time well spent. Lucky for me, people with injuries or muscle weakness, for example, can't dive into a rigorous physical routine at the get-go, so I have time to work on the mind from the beginning. You can do yoga lying in a hospital bed, even. It's very portable."

He smiled and the class laughed.

"Let me demonstrate a breathing technique that not only calms the nervous system, but helps to clear the body of cortisol, which is known to keep muscles from repairing themselves."

Ty demonstrated the technique and the students joined in. When his presentation was complete, he got a standing ovation. He blushed hotly as he returned to his seat, relieved and pumped up at the same time.

The next day, Ty went to his monthly session with Ron. As he sat down, Ron asked, "Hey, let's you drive the bus today, I've got a sore throat. What's on your mind?"

"You aren't contagious, are you?" Ty replied.

"Well, thanks so much for your caring concern. If you're nice to me, I promise not to cough on you."

"Fair enough," replied Ty. "Hope you feel better soon."

"Thanks", said Ron.

Ty decided to tackle the difficult subject Mac had dumped into his lap this semester. "I just finished Mac's trauma class." Ron nodded.

"Yes, Ron, as you probably already guessed we talked about RAD. Do you think I have RAD?"

Ron paused before speaking. "Ty, I'm not here to diagnose you. In fact, I am not a big fan of diagnoses. What matters is how you perceive yourself and your past. Remember, you have come a long way these past four years."

"I do see myself, or at least the way I used to be with my parents, as having some degree of RAD. At first it really freaked me out and I tried to block that idea out. But, Mac was really patient and we met a few times to work it out. He helped me see it clearly. The whole time I lived with my parents, it was one non-stop battle for control. I just always assumed they were too strict and too mean. I had to look out for number one because they never cared about what I wanted. I had a lot of anger and would argue and yell at them all the time, especially my mom."

Ty covered his face and rubbed his eyes. He removed his hands but kept his eyes closed. "I gave them hell. I never gave them a chance. I was too scared and too angry to ever give them a chance."

He paused and focused on his breathing for a couple breaths. "I've been getting flashbacks of stuff my mom used to do. Like, she used to do yoga in the living room while supper was heating up. I don't know, maybe it was to calm herself down so she wouldn't kill me, but, maybe," he looked intently at Ron, "she was trying to connect with me in a different way. A quieter way. She invited me often, but I only joined in with her a couple times, and I was always rowdy and disrespectful after a couple minutes."

"I can't believe how much I hated my mom growing up, and now I see how much she loved me." Ty choked back a sob, took a breath, and continued. "Now, every time I meditate or practice yoga, I see her, and I tell her I'm sorry. I tell her I'm practicing to honor her."

Ron broke in. "That's beautiful, Ty. Please remember, you were an innocent child with a horrible past to overcome. Most of your reactions were unconscious, purely and typically human responses to your trauma and how your brain and nervous system developed because of your experiences. Please don't spend any more time beating yourself up. As you know, my yoga master, it's not productive. Honoring your parents and yourself now, in the moment, is the best and ONLY thing you need to do."

Ty shook his head. "Yeah, I know. But I keep thinking of all the bad things I did, the hurt I caused."

After taking a long sip of his tea, Ron replied, "Use your mindfulness training to accept the thoughts, flashbacks, feelings, and gently let them go. Don't dwell on them or try to process them, just let them come and go. Eventually, you'll see them come up less often. Ty, your mom isn't looking for apologies or payback. She is over the moon with the wonderful person you have become. That is very healing for both your parents. Your growth into a kind, loving, happy, and competent person has far exceeded their expectations, and that is a rich reward for them."

Ty felt defensive. "Really, is that enough?"

Ron laughed warmly. "Oh my god, Ty, it's totally enough!" He took another sip of his tea to soothe his throat.

"Man, being a parent is a weird trip! You have to be a masochist to put up with everything!"

Ron countered, "Parents make a commitment, and adoptive parents in particular stand up in a courtroom in front of a judge and promise to care for the child for the duration. No money-back guarantee. Your parents made you a promise. Sometimes, that was all they could call upon to give them the strength to continue."

Ty whispered, "God damn." Then, he closed his eyes again to breathe.

Chapter 42: January

Ty entered Ron's office and dramatically shook his head around, causing a snow storm. Ron made an unpleasant face and brushed a few flakes off his pants.

"Yes, I know it's a blizzard out there and you get thirty points for trudging through the snow to come to therapy."

"Now we're talking. What do I get with my points?" Ty smiled, sitting down.

"Happiness and bliss."

Ty groaned.

"Ready to get down to work?" Ron queried.

Ty settled himself in and then looked at Ron.

"I want you to think of a baby you know, one or two years old."

"Yeah, my little cousin Gerry. He's awesome."

Ron nodded. "Close your eyes and really picture him. Tell me about him."

"I've watched him grow up from a newborn at the hospital to a little devil who can run around and really make some noise!"

They both laughed.

"He's the best, with soft, curly hair, huge eyes, and a big, drooly smile. I'm not really into kids, but Gerry decided he was gonna change all that. He loves to climb all over me. He loves it when I spin him around. When he first learned to stand up, you'd see his little hands grab the edge of the table, then he'd peek at you, all you'd see was his curly head and big eyes, but I knew just hidden below was his ginormous, proud, and drooly smile. It's impossible for me to be in a bad mood around that kid!"

Ty opened his eyes, waiting for Ron.

"If little Gerry were to be kidnapped right now and repeatedly mistreated for months on end, would you blame the little guy?"

Ty's eyes widened. "Hell, no, are you crazy, he's only two!?!"

"You and so many others who went through trauma blame yourselves. It's unconscious. It's fundamentally human, and it's the biggest source of your pain, your anger."

"Thank god I've gotten a handle on my anger," replied Ty.

"You have made tremendous gains, healing," Ron said with warmth in his voice. "Ok, homework exercise: when meditating, call up the baby you once were and send him compassion, forgiveness, healing. Picture yourself rescuing him from his captors, even if you have to pretend it's your cousin Gerry at first."

"I think I can do that."

"Of course you can. Try it every day until we meet up again."

It was clear the session was coming to a close, so Ron changed the topic.

"Hey, next month, we're going on a field trip, so you need to arrive fifteen minutes early."

"Where to? I'm not agreeing to anything without the details!"

"Fair enough. There's someone I want you to meet."

Ty shook his head. "Need more details…"

"Whatever happened to surprises?"

Ty laughed.

"Okay, we're going to a school where adults work to get their high school equivalency to meet the director, my buddy. He's a very muscular, bald, ex-con."

"Now you have my interest."

"Do I have your consent to accompany me on this life-changing field trip?"

"I suppose…" Ty laughed again, shrugging his shoulders.

On a frigid Thursday evening, Ty and Tasha drove back into town from a night at the movies. They re-hashed the film, arguing and laughing. "I can't believe you think the cop was a nice guy!" Tasha exclaimed. "He took all those bribes, he cheated on his wife… so what if he saved a couple people, that's his job! What about his core being? He's selfish, greedy…" Ty jumped in. "I know, I know, but he did risk his life on the bridge; he didn't have to." "I guess," Tasha conceded, "but I still think he got a charge out of being the hero."

All of a sudden, the car started to shudder and stall. "Did you run out of gas?" Ty asked. "No," Tasha replied, a little offended. She made several attempts to start the car, with no luck. Ty gave it a try as well with no success.

Ty silently cursed under his breath as Tasha called for a tow. He still had a couple hours of homework ahead of him. When she completed the call, she rejoined Ty and moved into him to keep warm. Ty started to open his mouth to complain, but he stopped himself. He drank in the scene: a quiet, snowy night with a beautiful woman snuggling into him for warmth. He closed his eyes and enjoyed his great fortune.

Chapter 43: February

Ty jumped into the passenger seat of Ron's car. "Okay, let's do it."

Ron nodded and they started on their way towards the school.

"So, Doc, how did you meet this character?"

"First off, he's a real human being, not a character, and second, I met him in prison."

"I always thought you had a shady past!"

"Funny. George was about a year from the end of his sentence when I was doing my face recognition research. He was already in a leadership position at the prison, mentoring and teaching the younger inmates."

"So you didn't turn his life around with your head shrinking skills?"

"Ha, ha. Actually, George taught me so much, he actually was one of my most influential mentors; he helped shape my career and my techniques."

"Wow. So, why do I need to meet him?"

"He has a life story similar to yours, and he's really cool. He's a boxer in his free time, and I'm sure he'd invite you to check out his gym if you ask him nicely."

"Cool. I'll definitely ask him. He's not going to be really bossy and preachy today, is he?"

"I doubt it. He wants to tell you his experiences and what has helped him in his life. It's up to you if you take his lessons to heart or not. All we can do is expose you to his ideas and approach to life."

Ron made a final turn and they parked in the lot.

The sign on the building read, 'Lifelong Learning Center', with an italicized saying underneath, 'It is never too late to learn and to grow'.

"George offers free counseling to all interested students, as well as teaching some of the courses himself. If you ever have some free time, he's always in need of volunteer tutors, hint, hint."

Ty tilted his head back, mouth open, groaning slightly.

The school appeared quiet. They found George alone in his office. He immediately rose to greet them, with a warm and welcoming smile despite his imposing figure.

"Come in, guys, so glad you could make it! Ty, I'm George. Welcome to our school."

"Thank you," Ty said, a bit shyly, but he managed to look George in the eyes.

"So, you heard about my past, you see that I've made some changes since doing my time."

Ty nodded, unsure of a reply.

As the three men sat down, each with a hot drink in their hand, George continued.

"I'm sure Ron wants you to hear about my childhood, don't you, Chief?"

Ron nodded, "Absolutely."

"My mother was a single parent, and an addict as well. She died of an overdose when I was four. I was abused not only by her, but by a long string of boyfriends, dealers, you name it. Physically and sexually. I was left alone a lot, when she went out for a hit or to find a new boyfriend. When she died, her first cousin adopted me. I had a loving adoptive family, blood relatives, but with all my anger, I gave them a rough time. I couldn't find peace, I was so upset about how my mother treated me, and then when she died I felt completely betrayed. Illogical, but a natural feeling, Ron tells me. Kids are hard-wired to be very self-centered, so they take everything personally. It wasn't until I found an exceptional therapist while in prison that I finally came to understand that my mother was the way she was regardless of me. She would have led the same life even if she never gave birth to me, her only child."

They all took a short pause to absorb the information.

"My adoptive mom, I call her Auntie, she loved me very much, but she was stretched thin. Five other kids, two jobs, and widowed at thirty-five. We practically raised ourselves, and not in a good way. I joined a gang, and I killed a teenage boy and, later, an older man who owned a gas station."
George took a deep breath.
"About five years into my sentence, I met a therapist named Thomas. He showed me how to own my anger and my grave mistakes. We decided on a plan of action. To seek forgiveness from the victims' families and to do good works to try to make up for my wrongs. Not that anything I could do would cancel out the murders. But at least to start being a force of good in the world."
They all sipped their drinks.
"So, I started teaching the younger inmates boxing, then history, then I started counseling them after I 'graduated' from therapy myself. As for the victims' loved ones, I wrote sincere letters of apology. One family completely ignored the letter, no reply. But the other, well, that's a different story. The father of the teenager had passed away by then, but his mother, she came to see me in person about two weeks after I mailed the letter. First, she cried, and I couldn't look at her. Then, we had a wonderful conversation. She said she had already forgiven me a few years back, and my letter was the confirmation that she was on the right path. She said she found so much peace after she forgave me. She took my hand and actually kissed it! We talked for about an hour, and she even came back to visit me every year. On the anniversary of her son's death. Since I've been a free man, I visit her more often, and she's like a second mom to me."
George was smiling, a look of calm on his face. It really caught Ty's attention.

"I'm married now, with a beautiful baby girl. Now, mind you, I could have easily hidden my past from my wonderful life partner, but I decided she needed to know the whole me, in order to have an honest and deep relationship. Not only did she meet my Auntie in short order, but my second mom as well. They are all best friends now, despite the huge age gap. I love it!"

George smiled again.

"My auntie, she's not well, so I check in on her every few days or so. She still hasn't forgiven herself for letting us kids run wild. She blames herself for how I messed things up. Each time, I beg her to let it go. To acknowledge that she did the best she could, that she loved us."

George's eyes welled with tears.

"I just hope she changes her mind before she passes on. I want her to heal, to have relief. I think my daughter is giving her some joy. Maybe we'll have a miracle."

"Has she tried yoga?" Ty offered.

George laughs. "Man, I wish. Once, I even tried to get her to try boxing, but no dice! Do you think you could show her some simple yoga, maybe like meditation?"

"I could try."

Ron looked at Ty. "That would be wonderful, Ty. If you're serious, you can ask George for his number and you two can make arrangements to visit his mom."

Ty nodded.

"Since I'm getting your number and all, could I see you work out at the boxing gym, too? I'm into all kinds of fitness. I'm a physical therapist, well, I will be official in June."

George shook his head enthusiastically. "Sounds like this will be a very symbiotic relationship. How's this Sunday for your first session in the ring? We can spend an hour with my mom first, so you two can break the ice, then try the yoga with her maybe the following week."

"I'm in," Ty said.

"One more thing," George added. "I am not trying to suggest that *you* have any sins you need to atone for, Ty. I just want you to see how I acknowledged my anger, and how I made the decision to let go of it. Amazing things starting happening to me once I did. I hear from Ron that you are well on your way. Please, keep up the good work and remember the payoff."

"Thanks, George. I mean it."

George laughed. "You bet."

They all shook hands and parted ways.

On Sunday at eleven am, Ty met George in front of his Auntie's house. He met this kind woman, they chatted for about twenty minutes, and then they made plans to meet again the following Sunday.

Next, it was off to the boxing club.

Ty took a private tour around the gym with George, then he watched him in a sparring session with a buddy. The workout and the techniques looked intense. The two men hugged each other and slapped each other on the back as they climbed out of the ring.

George took a long drink of water, then declared, "Your turn to get pulverized, Ty!"

Ty laughed, shaking his head. "I gotta warm up first."

"Don't worry, we'll go easy to get you ready."

Thirty minutes later, Ty was panting as he grabbed his water bottle.

George smiled. "You having fun?"

"No doubt." Ty pretended to be less exhausted than he actually was. His adrenaline was keeping him upright.

They both laughed.

"So, Ty, I thought you were a star football player. What are you doing walking around here like you're in awe or something?"

"Well, George, I used to think I was. Yeah, I had a great play my sophomore year and it got a lot of attention, but I wasn't pro material. I've come to realize I just like all things physical. And here, it's so alive, all the intensity, the sweat! And working out here it's not for the attention, it's not to build a career. It's just to enjoy it. No pressure on me."

"Well, you have a strong arm for a running back."

"You're gonna laugh, I have to give Ron the credit for that! Would you believe he forced me to do thirty minutes on the bag every day a couple summers ago? He made me send him 'before and after' photos of each workout!"

George bent over, laughing.

"That's my Ron! He sure gets creative in tailoring the therapy to the client! Anyways, you're welcome in here any time. I can think of a handful of guys that would like to spar with you."

"I can't afford a membership right now."

"You keep helping my momma and it's more than a fair trade! Plus, I hear you're a physical therapist?"

Ty nodded.

"If any guys want to ask you some questions, you'll give them advice?"

"Sure," Ty nodded, unable to keep the enthusiasm out of his voice.

"Should we call you 'Doc'?"

"Hell, no!" Ty replied, blushing.

"We'll see," laughed George, and he looked at his watch.

"Well, I hope you'll come back next Sunday if you can, after showing Auntie the meditation ropes."

"Sure, thanks!"

Ty was walking on air when he left the gym. He couldn't wait to tell Tasha all about his morning.

Tasha was studying at the kitchen table when Ty knocked on the door. "Can you give me another half hour, then I'm all yours." Ty nodded and took a book out of his bag. It was hard for him to be quiet, he had wanted to share his news with Tasha, but he knew better than to interrupt her. She always kept her word; when the work was finished, she gave Ty her complete attention and they always had fun.

When Tasha packed up her papers and shut down her computer, Ty went in full force. "Do you think boxers are sexy?" Tasha laughed. "No! They don't have any teeth and they treat their women bad." Ty laughed and poked her in the ribs. Then, he closed his lips over his teeth to pretend they were all knocked out. "Just give me one kiss, baby!" They laughed, and kissed, and moved it up to the bedroom.

The following Sunday, Ty made his way to George's aunt's house by himself. He would meet up with George at the gym afterward. He knocked at her door, tentatively at first, then a bit louder until he heard her call him in. "I'm in the bedroom, first door on your left," she called in a friendly tone.

The house was bright and sunny, but he almost tripped over a laundry basket on his way to her. "Are you okay, Ty? Sorry, my daughter is in the middle of doing my laundry, but she ran out to get some groceries."

Ty entered her room, now familiar. "Good morning, Mrs. Johnson," he said, with a nervous smile.

"Welcome, Ty, come in. Call me Mary. Have you had some breakfast?"

"I'm all set, thanks. You look wide awake today."

"I'm feeling good today, I might even make it out to the kitchen for lunch today!" she laughed, weakly, but with lively eyes.

Ty cleared his throat as he sat on the upholstered dining chair placed by her bed. "Have you done any meditating this week?"

"Oh, no, honey, I need more lessons!" she smiled.

"Okay, are you ready to start?"

They spent the next twenty minutes doing deep breathing and quieting the mind. Auntie seemed to be falling asleep.

Ty gently put his hand on her shoulder. She opened her eyes. "How did it feel?" Ty probed.

"I guess I did a lot of daydreaming. About when the kids were younger. Sorry, not much of a blank mind!"

"We can work on that next week. You've got the breathing and the quiet down pat, you're almost there," Ty replied.

"Tell me, son, why do you think I need this? I'd like to hear your opinion."

Ty hesitated, uncomfortable with the topic. "Well, George said you feel really badly that he got mixed up in a gang and kind of wrecked his life. I mean, before. Now he's got his act together."

"Yes," she replied, "but, of course, there's more. Things usually run deeper than just the surface. As you've heard, I wasn't home much to look after my kids, but when I was home, do you think I showed them love, caring, and guidance?"

Ty didn't know how to respond.

George's aunt smiled. "Well, I did. My entire life was about those kids. We snuggled together in bed, reading stories, we baked cookies from scratch, we even got to church a couple times a month!" she laughed.

After a brief silence, she continued. "Ty, what I would like you to understand is that as a mother, I took my role seriously and I loved all my kids equally, including George. And George, he was in bad shape when my cousin died. He needed lots of healing. I tried so hard to show him love, patience, and the right way to behave. He would have none of it. He would turn away from my hugs, my kisses, my attention. His anger was there from a young age. He wouldn't, couldn't let it go. A mother would do anything to heal her child. Despite all my efforts, he just couldn't take what I had to give." Tears welled up in her eyes. "So, of course I blame myself. A mother's love is supposed to move mountains!" She cried feely now. As uncomfortable as he was, Ty took her hand, but politely looked away.

Ty mustered all his strength to speak. "That must be how my mom feels, too." He took a deep breath and let out a quiet sigh.

She looked at him in the eyes. "Thank God Georgie's back for his mothering now. He takes such good care of me, fussing and coming over all the time. He's become a smart man, you know, he's taking his mom's love now before I'm gone and it'll be too late. I still believe, Ty, that a mother's love can move mountains… the child just has to be open to receive it." She smiled gently. "Can I have a hug?"

Ty hesitated for a moment, then approached her. Standing over her, he was unsure of how to position his torso without crushing her, but she showed him the way. He felt warmth and peace, so he closed his eyes. They breathed in tandem together for a dozen breaths or so, then a noise interrupted them.

It was George's, interrupting the intense moment. She entered the room and extended her hand. "Hello, you must be Ty. I'm Gloria, we're hoping you can zen our mom out!" she laughed and her mother did as well.

He smiled in reply, and held out his hand. "I'll be back next week, same time."

Ty then made his goodbyes, explaining that he was headed to meet George for a workout.

On a rainy Saturday morning, Ty found himself somewhere he never imagined… sorting clothes at the food bank. Tasha was handing out bags of groceries to the people who needed help, due to a job loss, an illness that put them into debt, mental illness, or addiction. She was very chatty with all who came, and Ty was impressed at how she could talk to anyone, and welcome them without judgment. Ty was glad he didn't have to be on the welcome wagon, though. He preferred to work in the back, and he felt just as productive, as there were huge piles of clothes to sort and bag up. Their college required forty hours per year of community service, and Ty was happy for the opportunity to do it with Tasha. He'd lucked out each year, getting his request to be placed with Shawn, and then Tasha.

When they left the building at the end of their shift, Tasha became pensive. "Some of the stories I hear, Ty, I mean, one day they're doing fine and the next their house gets taken away, they get laid off, it's all over." Ty nodded. "It's tough out there, from what I can tell." Tasha continued, "I plan to work even if I have kids, because what if my husband gets laid off, or dies? I can't support a family with no work history. Maybe I'll work part time when my kids are small, but I have to stay in the job market so my resume stays active. I'm not going to cross my fingers and hope my husband can float me for the next forty years." Ty got serious. "When you think of a husband, and kids… do I fit into that picture?" Tasha laughed. "Who else? Of course. If you'll have me." Ty blushed and turned to look at her. "I want to build a life with you, Tash. I'm not asking you to marry me right now, hell, I don't have two nickels to rub together and we don't have jobs lined up yet for after graduation, but I still hope we can spend our lives together." Tasha wiped away a tear, smiled, and gave Ty a big hug.

Chapter 44: March

Ty was one minute early for his meeting with Ron.

"Hey, eager beaver, did you miss me?"

"Of course," Ty laughed. "Let's make this a daily thing... not!"

They laughed again, each looking directly at each other in friendship.

"So, do tell, how was the boxing?"

"It's really fun. What a workout! We've sparred three times already. George's really good for an old timer."

Ron coughed and pounded his chest dramatically. "Old timer? He's ten years younger than me!"

They both laughed.

"I want to tell you about George's mom."

Ron nodded enthusiastically.

"She's really sweet. At first she didn't really understand what mediation is, and I could tell she was just following my directions to be polite. She tried really hard."

Ty paused.

"But our second time working together, something really cool happened. I decided to play a mantra with music, and after fifteen minutes or so with her eyes closed, she started to lightly shudder. Her eyes opened and she said it felt like a warmth moving through her chest and abdomen. I encouraged her to close her eyes again and clear her mind. A little while into it, tears started streaming down her face, but she didn't seem to notice. When we were done, she smiled and said she felt so relaxed. She made sure I promised to come again."

"Wow, Ty. That's huge! You are making an impact on the world and not even out of college yet."

Ty smiled.

Ty went to the store to find a birthday card for his dad. When he went back to the dorm, he was in an especially good mood, so he decided to write his parents a letter to send along with the card.

Dear Mom and Dad

Happy B day, Dad, I hope you have a great weekend with your buds. A little news from my world…

I'm going to graduate in Physical Therapy. They don't have a Sports Med major, and anyways, I realized I can really help people more in P.T. At first, I hated this assignment, stuck in a smelly nursing home, working with people coming out a stroke. But the progress they can make is really amazing. If they want it, of course. I'm assigned to one man and one lady who are both really motivated, Stan and Mrs. Tremont. Stan is pretty young, about 60 I think, so he's really motivated to get the hell out of there. He had retirement plans- golf, travel, new girlfriend. He's a riot. Mrs. T. is pretty old, but she has a truckload of family and friends who visit her constantly. They can't wait for her walking strength to come back so she can get back out on day trips with them again. She's really sweet. Once she got her speech back to normal speed, she hasn't stopped gabbing and she's taken me on as her "eleventh grandson". She's bummed that she can't cook for me, living in this prison, but we like to joke about what she would make for me as a thank you for helping her rehab. So far she's 'made' me cookies, ice cream sandwiches, and beef stroganoff!

Tasha and I are still together. She's someone I'm so proud to be with, and she always impresses me with her goals and her dive-in attitude. She's finishing up a great b-ball season, and she's doing student teaching. She plans to teach high school Gym and Health when she graduates. She says that's the best age because the younger grades aren't really focused. She taught elementary level last semester and didn't really like it. She loved the kids but wanted more of a challenge. We'll probably live together next year if we can get jobs in the same area.

Tasha thinks it's cute that I cook so healthy at her apartment. All she sees me eat on campus is burgers and pizza, so when I bust out the kale and the tofu like you guys made me eat all those years, she is shocked and impressed.

Looking forward to seeing you guys for Easter. I hope to see some scalloped potatoes, hint, hint!

Love, Ty

Chapter 45: April

On a blustery, rainy afternoon, Ty arrived soaking wet, but early.

"I heard it was gonna get even worse, so I got here early hoping we could get out a few minutes early?"

Ron chuckled. "We'll see… and, hello to you, too."

Ty gave Ron a salute and a greeting.

"We are nearing the end of our formal sessions. Time for some wrap up… I LOVE wrap up!"

Ty leaned his head back and groaned.

Ron rubbed his hands together… "Yes, that's when we verbalize what this was all about and what we've learned. Over these last two sessions we'll try to draw some meaningful conclusions. And, I have some information to disclose."

Ty's interest was piqued. "What information? Can you tell me now, please?"

"I'm getting there, Ty. You just walked in the door."

"Ok, ok."

Ron sat up straighter, ready for some work.

"Why exactly do you think your parents executed this four year plan?"

"Ron, we've been through this a million times."

"Humor me."

Ty sighed. "Because I hassled my mother for sixteen years and she wanted it to stop. She wanted me to go through counseling to get rid of my attitude and my anger."

Ron nodded. "Yes, but that is just part of the story. You're a legal adult now, and mature enough to think about your parents' side of the story. I'm going to disclose some information that your mother has authorized me to reveal when I felt you were ready. Please listen completely before jumping to conclusions…okay?"

Ty rubbed his forehead, then nodded, looking at Ron.

"The stress your mom endured while raising you was extremely high. I'm surprised myself that she didn't suffer from ulcers or worse."

"She sure went jogging a lot... Maybe that helped."

"I believe so. And a very supportive husband, good counseling, yoga, and lots of patience."

Ty nodded.

"Like we've talked about, it was very natural and normal for you to project your anger towards your birth mom onto your adoptive mom. The problem is that is very hard for a person to bear. She took it for sixteen years. Sometimes she felt like she was going insane. She often felt like a failure. Sometimes she felt so frustrated she wanted to run away and never come back. The dynamics you two had when you lived at home, was negative and extremely wearing."

"I know," said Ty. "I know better now. I'll never treat her like that again."

"That's wonderful, Ty. We're not trying to make you feel guilty, we just want you to understand this last facet of the picture. Your mom needed a partial break from relationship with you, meaning that you lived apart from them during your college years, to not only restore her peace and sanity, but her marriage as well."

"What? They're having problems?" Ty looked alarmed.

"No, Ty, what I mean is that their marriage took a back seat for sixteen years. Your parents wanted some calm and privacy so they could reconnect and heal their bond. And enjoy it. I believe they just had a great time in Hawaii, for example."

Ty interrupted, "They were happy to send me away to college?"

"Yes, and do you believe that if someone put their needs on hold for sixteen years, they deserve to call the shots for a while?"

"Yeah, I can't argue with that."

Ron smiled.

"The goal was about changing the family dynamics and healing. Over these last few years, you three have made some tremendous changes for the better in the way you communicate, interact, and trust one another."

Ty remained silent, waiting for Ron to continue.

"What would you say your new relationship with your parents is like?"

Ty took a moment to think. "Kind of like between three adults, three friends."

Ron smiled again. "I like that, Ty… do you?"

"Yes."

"Now, back into the rain with you, my drowned rat!"

They laughed, and Ty gave Ron a quick hug as they both rose to leave.

Still in the spirit of the counseling session Ty just left, he decided to write one last letter as a college student, to his parents. He would mail it off with one of the invitations furnished by the college.

Dear Mom and Dad,

Here is my graduation invitation… pretty classy, hey? I can't believe I'm going to graduate in three weeks. That's crazy. Tons of work to finish, but I know I'm going to graduate! Ha ha. I'm counting the days until you come for graduation. I want my parents there to share in the proudest day of my life.

Mom, I'm so sorry to hear what you went through, while raising me. I understand now that you were tired of my attitude, and my anger, and it hurt you and Dad. I never meant to hurt you. You are the best mom. You always kissed me good night, and I imagine many times you wanted me out of your life, but you kept your promise and never gave up on me. You read me stories, always asked me about my day, and we cooked together. I have a lot of good memories of your love.

As I headed off to college, you needed space to take a break from it all,
and you wanted me to have a chance to make changes in my thinking
and my heart. You kind of forced me, but in the end I am very glad.
I eventually stopped resenting your counseling order. Ron has been
really cool. I learned a lot from him and made some good changes.
You have given me a good life and you will be proud of me.
Love, Ty

Ty handed Ron an envelope.

"I hope you can come to my graduation."

"I'm there! Of course, Ty. I wouldn't miss it."

"Maybe someday when you screw up an ankle or a knee on the basketball court I'll be your P.T."

"Payback is sweet, isn't it?"

They both laughed.

"But really, I do hope you will always feel free to contact me, even when you're rich and famous. And I can always use someone to mop the floor with me at hoops... to keep me humble."

"Thanks," Ty replied.

"Hello, Mrs. John... I mean Mary," Ty said cheerfully when he entered Mary's room for their weekly meditation session.

"Why, good morning, Ty, it's wonderful to see you. What are we working on today?"

"Well, I have a nice yoga nidra guided meditation that I'd like to try. It takes about twenty minutes. Why don't we practice our breathing together first? In through the nose, out through the nose... let's do that for about five minutes together. Close your eyes and listen to your breath. If you get distracted and start thinking of other things, try to bring your attention back to your breath. You ready?"

Mrs. Johnson smiled, "Sure, just tell me when to close my eyes."

They sat in stillness together, listening to their breathing. Ty always had a hard time quieting his mind, until he fell upon the technique of literally listening to the sounds his breathing makes.

When approximately five minutes had passed, Ty put his hand lightly over Mary's to signal that they were done. Once she opened her eyes, Ty spoke again.

"You did great! How did it feel?"

"Well, I did keep having a lot of thoughts, but I think I did pretty good listening to my breath, and the thoughts passed by. I actually think I can try that on my own... How often should I do it, Ty?"

"Great!" Ty was enthused. "It's not about how often, but when... Sometimes you may feel you need it are when you are starting to think about things that make you sad, such as regrets, and when you are trying to fall asleep. At least a few times a day would be great."

"I think I can do that!"

"Okay, let's try that guided meditation I told you a little about. I will have you close your eyes, breathe in and out through just your nose like we were doing before, then just stay focused on what I say during the whole meditation time." Mrs. Johnson closed her eyes and started breathing evenly. Ty verbally guided her through a series of things to pay attention to, such as parts of her body in a sequence, her breath in and out, and lastly a visualization of a very peaceful setting with the light ocean breeze, blue sky, and warming sun. He ended the session by asking her to slowly start moving her fingers and toes, to gently massage her face with her fingertips, and to acknowledge the beauty inside of her.

"Ty, you are such a wonderful boy, you bring me such peace!"

Ty blushed. "You have worked very hard, I can't take that credit. I hope this brings you comfort in the days to come. I can still come for a few more weeks, until graduation, so we can practice together."

Ty no longer felt uneasy hugging Mary. He initiated the goodbye hug himself this week.

As Ty left the Johnson home, he felt very peaceful himself. He felt more sure than ever that he wanted to continue integrating yoga and meditation into his physical therapy career. It felt right.

Chapter 46: May

On a cold but sunny morning in early May, Ty jogged over to Tasha's apartment. "You're early," she said with a smile. They kissed, hugged, then Ty went over to the sink to wash his hands. Since they had discussed the menu yesterday, each knew their tasks and they set about working on the picnic food. "Are you sure Mac wants me tagging along? I'm sure he wants to spend some time with you since we're leaving soon, after graduation." Ty shook his head. "No, babe, he loves you. We'll have fun!" Mac was not moving on after graduation; he had two more years of his graduate program and teaching contract. Ty hoped he and Tasha would not be moving too far from the University. He'd like to remain close with Mac.

"Hey," Ty said, "did I tell you Shawn has a new flame? They're both going to work for the pharmaceutical lab, two science geeks in love!" Tasha turned to him, smiling. "I'm so glad. Is it Trina? I really like her... tell me it's her!" Ty looked up at the ceiling. "I think so. It's either Trina, or Tina, or Mina, or Sheena, I forget." Tasha jumped on Ty's back, "You brat, I'm gonna get you for playing with me!" She giggled, "Just tell me it's Trina, or I'm gonna tickle you!" Ty took hold of Tasha's legs so she could stay on his back. He ran around the house like a horse with her as the rider. They both laughed, Tasha got down, and they kissed for a long time. "Promise me you'll let me follow you wherever you go," Ty said, a serious look on his face. "You think I'm gonna let you out of my sight?!" Tasha laughed. They kissed again, then started packing the food into her car.

As Ty started to transfer the food from Tasha's car to Mac's van, he could hear the good natured ribbing and laughing between his girlfriend and Mac. He knew Tasha would feel included in short order. Mac drove them to a pond and bog with picnic tables overlooking the water, which was filled with lily pads. The flowers hadn't bloomed yet, but the buds held promise, of pink and white blossoms in just a few weeks. Mac wiped his mouth with a napkin, saying, "That was delicious! Especially the fruit salad, thank you! I want to be the first to say to you both how proud I am of you kids, that you are graduating, that you both found your career calling, and that you have already started to make a difference in your respective fields." Ty blushed. "Man, come on!" Mac waved his hand dismissively. "Ty, you have come so far. From an angry freshman to a beautiful young man who not only found peace with himself but is bringing it to others. You blow me away!" Tasha's eyes welled with tears. "Don't I deserve any of the credit?" she teased. "All the way, Tasha! You are so good for my boy. You two make a great team." They all sat quietly for a while, basking in the compliments, the friendship, and the gentle warmth of the sun.

Ty broke the silence. "I'm gonna miss you, man. What do you think about us opening a practice together after you get your PhD?" Mac laughed. "Are you a mind reader or something?! We can collaborate in the future; the time isn't right for either of us yet. But, man, it would be cool! We could open a holistic center, where I do the counseling, you do the physical therapy and yoga, mediation, crystal shakra healing, past-life regression, high colonics, shaman work, kale smoothies..." Ty punched Mac in the arm. "Hey, quit making fun of me!" Mac retorted, "Dude, it makes me happy to make fun of you, can't you let me enjoy life a little?" Ty nodded, all the while rolling his eyes. He was in a fantastic mood and very optimistic about his future.

Ron sat on the edge of his seat.

"Have your parents responded to your invitation? Are they coming to the ceremony?"

"No... No answer yet. I should call them in case it got lost in the mail."

"Absolutely...So, what makes you think your parents are going to show up at the graduation?"

"Because we got along fine at Easter."

Ron sat silently, waiting for Ty to elaborate.

"What do you want from me, Ron?"

"I want to wrap this up, to hear you utter the golden nugget."

Pause.

Ty took a breath and continued. "I know they will be front and center at my graduation. I know it as sure as I'm alive here sitting in this chair."

"Sounds like you now believe they love you more than anything. That they are proud of you and so thankful that you are their son."

"Yeah."

Ron let his eyes well up with tears.

"Stop it, man. Don't be a sissy."

Ty got up and opened his arms to Ron. They hugged each other for a few moments, then moved apart.

"Sissy owes me a burger and a beer, right now, I'm starving. This session is OVER!"

"That's my boy!" Ron patted his shoulder as they headed out the door.

AFTERWORD

June 5

Dear Ron,

I can't thank you enough for what you've done for our son. Instead of taking credit, you said that it has been an extremely enriching experience. Your patience, generosity, and open heart made all the difference.

What Paul and I hoped for most out of this experience were healing and peace for our son. We see clearly that he is well on his way, already reaping the benefits of a calmer soul. We see him enjoying emotional closeness in his relationship with Tasha. The level of trust and mutual respect they seem to share has come about because Ty chose to fully participate in this growth journey.

Graduation day was wonderful. We are so proud of our son. I am now able to comfortably and even eagerly look into his beautiful face, his eyes. I hadn't been able to do that for a very long time. That is the most precious gift I will ever receive.

With much love,
Terry

Made in the USA
Middletown, DE
24 April 2017